FIFT'
SPLIT

An urban adventure for three well to do businessmen,
and a new start in life for two men down on their luck...
... that's if all goes well.

Roger Roberge Rainville

Fifty-Fifty Split

ISBN: 978-1-945423-09-3

Copyright © 2018 by Roger Roberge Rainville

All rights reserved. No part of this publication may be reproduced, distributed, or transmitted in any form or by any means, including photocopying, recording, or other electronic or mechanical methods, without the prior written permission of the publisher, except in the case of brief quotations embodied in critical reviews and certain other noncommercial uses permitted by copyright law. For permission requests, write to the publisher, addressed "Attention: Permissions Coordinator," at the address below.

Five Stones Publishing (ILN)
Permissions Manager:
randyjohnson@ilncenter.com
www.ilncenter.com
Printed in the United States of America

Disclaimer

FIFTY-FIFTY SPLIT is a fictional urban adventure story with actual locations found in New York City, and some, created by the author. The players' names used in this tale were made up. Any similarity to names of actual people who are alive or have lived is purely coincidental.

Dedication

I dedicate this book to my wife Donna, my children; Linette and Christian, to my grandchildren, Saralin, TJ, Isaac and Evan and to my great grandchildren, Emma and Ethan. May you all pursue your dreams and accomplish all that you make up your mind to do, and succeed in it, thus leaving a lasting legacy.

God's best to you...I love you

Acknowledgements

I'd like to thank Kathy Aures, Randy Johnson, Monique Rainville, Margie Weber and Donna Rainville for proof-reading and editing this story. It was invaluable. I also thank Cheryl Graham from the Seneca Nation Language School in Irving New York for her contribution with regards to Seneca language terms I wanted to use for some of John "Hawk" Hawkeye's dialogues.

Forword

Interesting facts about this book

The idea for this story started in 1976 and lay dormant until 2017. It began with about fifty or so hand-written notes that were put aside for forty-one years and didn't come to fruition until 2018.

Back when I got the idea to write it, I only had a typewriter and didn't really know how to type, still don't. I use the "search and peck" system. So, as you can imagine, besides trying to fix a thousand typos and doing "cut and paste," it would have been a literal nightmare had I not had a computer.

Having worked with computers as a teacher from 1991 to 2014, I learned enough about them so I could use a word processing program to write, save, and edit my work. Without that, Fifty-Fifty Split and my other books would have never been written.

Also, there were no "high tech" cell phones back then, which is the main mode of communication in the story. Being from the Baby Boomer generation and growing up using rotary dial telephones, today's cell phone systems are a marvel to me.

I needed to do a lot of research for this project. One of the hardest things I had to do was, getting several Seneca language terms that I could use for some of Hawk's remarks. It is a very interesting language. I need to thank Cheryl Graham from the

Seneca Nation Language School in Irving for her help in giving me several terms that are used in the story.

I also did a lot of online searches about New York City; Times Square, the Pedestrian Mall, streets names, parks, police precincts, hospitals and the bus terminal. Although it was tedious and time consuming trying to find certain information, online research made gathering material fairly easy. Having the internet at my disposal, I was able to navigate through parts of the City of New York and find ideal locations for some of the scenes.

Chapter 1

Rich and bored

This story begins with Jacques Blanchard, a 46 year old man from Montreal, Québec who studied fashion and design in Paris when he was in his early twenties. He came up fast in the world of fashion and set up his own garment company ("Jolietoile") in Manhattan's Garment District. He's been in that industry for the last twenty years and does business with fashion outlets in cities throughout the United States, Canada, and Europe.

It is early spring. Jacques is in a limo that's taking him to his office on 9th Avenue from his Chelsea Park area apartment. Although he's seen this many times before, today, the presence of several beggars with outstretched hands toward passersby annoys him. On a few occasions, he has given some of them a couple of dollars or whatever coins he had in his pocket.

Today, for some unknown reason, he's more aware of this phenomenon of begging for cash and says to himself, "What is it with these people begging for money day in and day out? If they're able to go out panhandling, surely they could work and stop pestering people!"

He arrives at his building and takes the elevator up to his office; it's at the very top of this twenty floor high rise. He loves the view and spends some time everyday looking over the city. He keeps powerful binoculars in his desk that he uses to look at certain activities that catch his eye. He's seen many interesting things from up there; accidents, police chasing individuals on foot or by car, fire trucks, emergency vehicles trying to rush through traffic, people arguing, kissing, fighting, making drug buys, and even some…getting extremely amorous on roof tops. He'll tell you that he's seen just about anything you can imagine from that perch.

In his cozy, luxurious office, he goes about his daily routine. His days are usually filled with answering or making phone calls; some are local while some are to different parts of the US or other countries like Canada, Mexico, England, France, and Italy. Other duties that occupy him are; meeting with clients, signing contracts and making phone contacts with magazine people and stores that sell his goods. His tasks do not change much from day to day.

Today will turn out to be a bit different for him. He pauses to evaluate his daily routine and thinks about all that he's accomplished. He reaches in his pocket and takes out his money clip, peels off a one hundred dollar bill from among the singles, tens, twenties …and grins. He could live very comfortably off his savings for the rest of his life, with plenty left over after leaving this planet.

His thoughts turn to his business and how it has become somewhat mundane. He realizes that his life lacks excitement. The most he's known for the past ten years has come in the form of parties his wife Margo has given for their elite friends. Deep down, he knows that he's a basic man, and although his fortune is appreciated, he needs more out of life than parties and social events with people he doesn't particularly enjoy. He'd love to take time off to enjoy something different, something new and exciting.

He further reasons that his right hand man, Don Blake, knows just as much about the company as he does and that he could actually manage things should he decide to take time off. Don is 38, and married with four kids. He's the typical family man and very dedicated to them and his job. Generally, he's a no-nonsense kind of person; an above average, good man.

Jacques is dying to do something completely new and different that would add a little spice to his life, but nothing comes to mind at the moment. He pauses, *What could I do that'd be exciting? I've done everything I've ever wanted to do and don't care to repeat any of it. There must be something out there that would top everything I've done so far…but what?*

He gets up from his desk and goes to the window to look outside. He glances around, first at the top of the buildings, then his gaze slowly goes down to the streets. He watches the ant-size forms scurrying about below and says out loud, "What do all of you people down there do for excitement?"

As he continues scanning the people, he zeros in on a couple of guys mingling with the rest of the pedestrians. He can see them with hands outstretched toward passersby. Some people stop to give a few coins or a dollar bill, but most just ignore them.

This makes him think of the Beatitudes: *"Blessed are the poor, for yours is the Kingdom of God."* And.., *"Blessed are ye that hunger now: for ye shall be filled."*

Then he thinks, *Man, these aren't poor people! They're bums! They're just lazy! What has brought them to that kind of existence? What sad lives they lead.*

His thoughts are interrupted when he sees a couple of beggars converging angrily on one of their own. He quickly grabs the binoculars from his desk and gets back to the window to see what's going on. He sees a couple of bums trying to get something out of the hand of another man, possibly a couple of dollar bills or a five. What he sees intrigues him!

"My God!" he says to himself. "Those bums are like a bunch of vultures on a carcass! What would they do to him if he had a hundred dollar bill?"

He watches the scuffle until one of the bigger men punches the bill holder in the face and rips the cash from his hands. The people passing by look in disgust and continue on their way. They want no part of that scene. The little man is lying on the ground bleeding profusely from his nose.

A slight distance away, a lone policeman sees the commotion and yells at the group to break it up! Given that he's alone, he's careful in dealing with the "perps." He thinks it more prudent to approach them with caution. As he nears, the two thieves scatter among the people on the sidewalk and blend in. He was a bit too late to stop the victim from having his nose broken and his money stripped from him. What could he do? ...shoot the big guy? ... shoot them both... for the little bit of money involved?

He mumbles to himself, "I wish these guys weren't out here bothering people for money; what a mess!"

Even if he arrested the man guilty of punching the other, the city would then have to house, feed and prosecute him. That's time and money! The city jails are full enough and the brass would rather reserve the cells for the likes of rapists, thieves, murderers and drug dealers.

The officer approaches the forty something bloodied beggar who is still on the ground and asks him if he'd like to go to the hospital.

The teary-eyed, beat up and very angry man yells at the cop, "NO! I don't want to go to no damn hospital! Where the hell were you when they were beating me up!? Damn it! They took my ten dollars! I want it back!"

The cop is surprised, *"Ten bucks! That was a real good score for this guy."*

Apparently, his appearance and manner of begging touched a soft-hearted pedestrian who gave him a ten dollar bill. His problem was that a couple of other beggars saw it, and attacked him. Ten bucks is a pretty good score when you're homeless and count on donations to buy daily necessities...whatever that entails; could be booze or cigarettes. Street people usually don't buy food with what they collect from kind folks. For that, there's always some charitable mission nearby where they're able to eat for free.

Anyway, I guess the pain from the punch in the nose hadn't registered yet. There's blood all over his face and coat. You'd think that would take priority over the money he lost.

The officer says, "Take it easy buddy! We'll get you an ambulance."

"I don't need no damn ambulance!" he says angrily. "I need my money! Those rats! I'll kill them! I'll kill 'em both!!!

He struggles to his feet with the help of the officer, shrugs him off and begins walking in the direction of his attackers. The cop knows that there's nothing he can do.

He shakes is head, *This poor demented fool is going to get another beating!*

To the cop, this guy is just another alcoholic who can't think straight anymore and no one can reason with him. All he knows is that they stole his money; money for another drink of whiskey or wine. He's just another drunk who lives from day to day for his next fix!

Having a soft spot in his heart, he calls out to the guy and tries once more to get him to go for medical attention. "Hey come on back here. You've got to go to the hospital! You're bleeding all over yourself!" Good effort, but to no avail. He certainly can't follow him to make sure he won't get beat up again. He yells at him as he walks away, "They're gonna beat you up again! Just let it go!"

It's no use, the officer's advice is ignored and the poor guy staggers down the street. Perhaps he'll find his assailants, but what then? For sure he's not going to get his money back, just another beating, or even worse, he could lose his life. This poor soul is stubborn. Another man might have walked away or had taken the offer to go to the hospital, but for this individual, common sense just isn't part of his mental capacity.

Everything is over and Jacques goes back to his desk thinking to himself, *Life in the big city! Man, oh man! What a jungle!*

Chapter 2

Idea for an adventure

After working for about an hour, Jacques' thoughts come back to the bums and what he witnessed. His creative mind comes up with an idea... *What if I gave one of those bums a hundred dollars in cash? Wouldn't it be interesting to see what would happen if some of the other bums found out about it?*

He can't even imagine what could develop. Another thought comes to mind, *What if it was a thousand dollars?*

Suddenly, he's got his adventure! His imagination runs wild and he begins visualizing all sorts of scenarios. He realizes that it'll take a few days for him to put this together and calls his assistant to come to his offices. Don comes in and waits for whatever he's been summoned to do.

IDEA FOR AN ADVENTURE

Jacques says to him, "I'm going to take off a few days, maybe a week, and I want you to take charge of things while I'm gone. Do you feel you're up to it?"

"Of course!" he replies. "No problem at all Mr. Blanchard. I'll be just fine."

"Great!" says Jacques. "Starting today, handle all my incoming and outgoing calls, cancel any meetings I have with whoever might be on my schedule and reschedule for next week."

It was done! Jacques was now free to fully develop his adventure.

He starts thinking a little more about the whole thing and reasons, If I just gave a bum a hundred dollars, there's nothing adventurous doing it that way. To make this a really interesting situation, it has to be much more than a hundred dollars! How much shall it be, and who should I choose to be the recipient of such a gift?

It's 11 am. He spends the rest of the morning and part of the afternoon writing ideas down on paper. For what he's got in mind, he'll need help and thinks about asking two very close friends of his if they'd be interested in his adventure. After a few hours of planning, he's ready to go forward with it. The amount he has in mind isn't a hundred dollars or a thousand, it's *two hundred thousand dollars*! Some more planning and preparation will be needed, but he has exactly what he wants. He's anxious to get this in motion. He plans on having everything and everybody in place within three days.

The plan

He plans on contacting a good friend of his, Dexter Druitt, at the Businessmen's Finance Bank on 9th and 20th and have him draw up a two hundred thousand dollar cashier's check. He'll make arrangements to have that cash amount on hand to cover the check. Then, two vagrants are to be chosen; one from the north end of Manhattan and another from the south end. Each will be given half of the check and specific written instructions as to how they are to proceed in order to get their reward for participating.

The help he has in mind for this adventure are his friends, Rick Gage and Sergio Malick. Rick is 45 year old and owns a large import/export fabric company called "Fibers & Fabrics." He provides a lot of material for Jacques' fashion and design needs.

Jacques is certain he'd love the idea. His wife Joan busies herself with a number of meaningless elite organizations. He loves her and lets her occupy her time with her little groups. They have two children.

His other friend Sergio is 47 years old. He's a building contractor who owns a large construction company called, "Sermack Construction. He's built several large high rise buildings in the city and owns a couple of dozen older ones, and warehouses as well. He's one of New York's top money men.

He's divorced from Marla, but is on good terms with her. Now, he's leading a life of a playboy. His main interests are; fishing, golf, socializing with friends, and being the best he can be in his business.

Jacques knows Sergio would be up for this too. He's adventurous and a bit wild! As a matter of fact, he's sure that Sergio would be miffed if he were not included. All three know each other very well and belong to the same country club along with their wives; even Serge's ex-wife, Marla, is a member. The three friends play racket ball every week and the conversation often ends up being about having something new and exciting in their life, but they never come up with anything. That's about to change.

Jacques calls his two buddies and explains what he plans on doing. After giving them a few details, they think it'd be a fun thing to do! He tells them that he's going to hire eight trusted men that will take on the task of following, or shadowing the two subjects.

They will feed the CREW (Jacques, Sergio and Rick) information on the vagrants' progress via two-way communication devices; sleeve microphones and earpieces. Also, they will use their cell phones for streaming videos to them so they can be closer to the action. This will be crucial.

The two subjects being tailed will be wearing New Orleans Saints caps and be given a slightly oversized Saint Christopher medal on a chain to wear around their neck that will have an "S5 Poor Man's LoJack" tracking chip and a tiny "Electret Condenser" mic in it. They'll need to protect those as much as their half of the check …and keep them well hidden at all times.

Chapter 3

Picking up a vagrant

The next step will be finding two vagrants. Jacques calls a police captain friend of his (Captain Dave Durso) in one of the south side's precincts and another captain of a north side precinct (Captain Edward Bates). He only knows the latter through a sergeant friend named Frank who works at that precinct.

Both captains are told that he wants to do a social experiment and needs a vagrant from each precinct that he could secretly observe. Jacques gives them a thousand dollars each for setting it up. He tells the captains to pick up a vagrant in their district and hold him in their jail until noon the next day.

Captain Bates of the north precinct is an overbearing, portly, pot-belly guy who doesn't always do things by the book. Even as a cop, he'll bend the law if it's to his advantage. He's a harsh leader who demands that his officers jump when he says, "jump!"

He picks the team of Lance Weber and Antonio Perez to do the job of picking up the north side vagrant. Weber is a white man, age 29, and Perez, a 27 year old Hispanic.

The order is given in the captain's office…on the QT.

Officer Weber asks the captain, "What the hell are we going to arrest a bum for? We got to charge him with something! What? We'll bring him in and the judge will let him go as soon as he steps into the court room!"

"Ya think I don't know that?" Bates replies. "Just do as you're told and get me a flipping bum, okay?"

Sarcastically, Weber says, "Sure Captain. You got a color preference or will anybody do?"

"WHAT?" says Bates?

"I mean, you want a Black, Hispanic or White bum?"

He snaps back, "Look! If you two don't hit those streets and bring me a bum, any bum… I'll have you walking a beat instead of riding that nice cushy patrol car!"

Hurriedly, the officers leave the station and go off in search of a bum. Perez says under his breath, *"Great assignment! ¡Qué tontería! Eso es estúpido!"* (What nonsense! This is stupid!)

CRUISING THE STREETS

It's about 7:30 pm when Perez and Weber begin patrolling in the area of 126th and Douglas near the Apollo Theatre. They're certain there'll be quite a few street people hanging around and should be able to find a man that fits the bill.

After about fifteen minutes into the search, Perez says, "Hey look! There's one!"

"Why a white bum? Why not a Hispanic bum?" asks Weber.

Perez answers, "What the hell man! The captain wants a bum, so there's a bum!"

"Yeah, well Chico, there's a Hispanic one right over there in the doorway of that closed store. Let's get him! He looks like more of a bum than the WHITE guy!"

"Very funny," says Perez. "Let's just get a bum, any bum okay amigo?"

Weber says, "I got an idea. Let's forget these two and let's bag us an Indian! That way, I won't hurt your feelings about the 'Hispanic bum' thing. How's that, my rice and bean-eating partner?"

Perez gives him a cold look and says, "Up yours white meat! But okay, let's grab us an Indian! Man, I'd still like to know why we're doing this! It doesn't make any sense. It's a waste of time!"

Weber says, "You know as well as I do, orders is orders! Let's get it over with!"

As they continue to cruise around, Weber finally spots a man and exclaims, "Look there! Is that an Indian?"

Perez laughs and mocks him, "Just because the man is wearing a headband don't mean he's Indian! Idiota! He's just some goofy hippy type. He'll do though."

Weber comes back with a bit of an attitude in his voice, "Yeah! The hell with you! He's a White guy. I knew you'd try to do that! We're going for an Indian! What part of 'Indian' did you not understand, hombre?"

"Yo! Chill out, Web! I'm only kidding! We'll find our man. Just keep driving… and have another doughnut, Gordito!" (Fatso!)

PICKING UP A VAGRANT

After about a half hour of driving around, Perez says, "Finally, there he is! Our Indian! Are you happy now?"

"Yup!" Replies Weber. "I'm happy as a pig in mud!"

Perez says, "¡Aye…madre de Dios! ¡Qué grande! He's a big man, man! Since you're quite a bit bigger than me, you go get him!"

Weber fires back, "Do I look stupid to you?! How about you and me go get him? We're a team, remember?"

They stop, get out of the squad car and approach their target. Perez walks up to him first and asks what his name is.

"Hawk," he replies.

Perez says, "Is that a nickname or your birth name?"

"It's my nickname."

Weber tells him, "Okay, let's see some ID!"

"I don't have any ID, man! Somebody on the street lifted my wallet about a month ago. I have no ID."

Perez says, "You're under arrest!"

"What the hell for?" says Hawk.

Perez replies, "Oh, that'd be a 10-39Q or something like that…vagrancy, I think!"

He gets angry and says, "Are you're CRAZY! What kind of BS is this!? You can't arrest me for some goofy charge like that!!! Don't you guys have something better to do than hassle me? I'm not doing anything wrong."

Weber finally puts in his two cents and tells him to get in the car. As they both grab an arm, Hawk shakes them off and after about half a minute of scuffling, they take him to the ground and cuff him. He relaxes, walks quietly to the car and gets in without causing any more trouble. He has that look of a very tired, worn out man.

Both officers are glad it was that easy. Hawk is big.... and strong! He could have hurt them both if he wanted to, but didn't want any part of being charged with…"assaulting an officer." That would be a very big mistake.

He's taken to the station and placed in a cell for the night. He knows they don't have anything on him and figures that maybe they just arrested him to meet some quota so that it looks good on their arrest tally sheet. Still, he's a bit nervous, seeing that there's a warrant out for him on the other side of the state. He's really beat and needs to get a good night's sleep. The cell will provide that. He figures he'll deal with the bogus charge in the morning.

He does have ID. He hid his wallet in a special place once he got to the City. He was warned about pickpockets and if he ended up in a shelter; that someone could go through his personal items while he slept. Smart move! What's more, the cops won't be able to do a search on his background. In the morning, he plans on telling the judge that he came from an orphanage in northern New York that is now closed, and he has no family that he knows of.

Chapter 4

Hawk's background

John "Hawk" Hawkeye (Proud Seneca Indian in his early 30s) comes from the Cattaraugus Indian Reservation in Irving, New York near Gowanda. He has a small house on Route 438, also known as "4 Mile Level Road." It's about 35 to 40 miles south of Buffalo. He's married to a lady named Diana. They have a nine year old boy named Jacob.

He has a "Charles Bronson" way about him. He's six foot four, quiet, and fairly mild-mannered. He's never looked for trouble, but …he's the kind of man that if you disturb his peace or corner him, the giant in him rises up, and you may need to get out of his way.

Hawk had to flee the reservation after being involved in a bar fight that wasn't his fault. He ended up in New York City's upper Manhattan area. It all started after a hard day's work on a building in the city of Buffalo. He and a couple of his friends, Little Joe, and Martin (structural steel fitters) went to unwind at the Malamute Bar located on South Park, in the Old First Ward. As they were quietly chatting and drinking a few beers at a table, five guys from another construction crew (not locals) who were standing at the bar, began cracking jokes about Indians.

Hawk and his friends took it for awhile, but Little Joe couldn't let it go any longer. He made a move to confront the five men; Hawk grabbed his arm as if to say, "Sit down." He said to him in his Seneca native tongue, *"Sënöh nësye:h... snônos!"* (Don't do it... be cool!)

Little Joe slowly sat back down. The guys at the bar laughed at him when they saw him retreat, then kept up the abuse. After about ten more minutes of insults, Hawk says, "Ha'degaye:i" (That's enough!)

He stood up, walked over to the guy spewing out most of the insults and told him, "Why don't you and your buddies stop bugging me and my friends? We've had a hard day on the job and are just trying to chill out. We're not bothering anybody. Just leave us alone, okay?"

The bar had about ten of its regulars. They all turned to watch what was going to happen next.

The loud mouth said to Hawk, "Me and my buddies don't want you Indians in here! Why don't you and the other two yahoos there leave and go back to the reservation and do a rain dance or something!"

His buddies all laughed...and Hawk said, "You think that's funny, eh? Tell you what. Next idiot in this little girly group makes a stupid comment I'm gonna slap him like a bad kid! You find that funny…moron?!"

One of the morons replied, "Are you crazy man?! There are five of us! We'll trash you and your pals, then, throw your sorry butts out of here!"

Hawk stands back a bit with his arms downward, palms open, and says, "Okay! I REALLY don't want any trouble, but if you insist on hassling us, you can make your move anytime you're ready, white trash!"

At that moment, the man nearest Hawk threw a beer in his face and the other four rushed in, knocked him to the floor and started punching and kicking. Little Joe and Martin made their move to help by taking two attackers off him. With his size and strength, he managed to free one hand and punched one guy square in the nose. That put him out of commission. He got up and threw another guy into a wall, face first. That put a very nasty cut over his left eye. He then picked up the remaining attacker and tossed him over the bar where he ended up crashing into the stock shelf and destroyed numerous bottles of liquor. After that, he turned and kicked a guy who was on top of one of Martin with his steel-toed boot. He got him right in the ribs and heard the man groan in pain...probably broke his ribs. Another bad guy had Little Joe in a rear choke hold. He back handed him so hard that he staggered backward onto the juke box and smashed the glass with his elbow, then dropped to the floor, unconscious. The other two punks beat it out the door. The whole brawl took about two minutes. By this time, the bartender had called 911.

An old hippy kind of guy approached Hawk and said, "Yo dude! The bartender called the cops. You better split, man!"

Hawk said, "Why should I split? I didn't start it! They did!"

The hippy replied, "It don't matter man! They're busted up and you're not! They'll press charges and you'll be screwed, man! You gotta go dude! Go!"

Hawk reasoned that the hippy was right. He gathered his boys and took off. They all headed back to the reservation and checked out the news on TV to see if it became a police matter. Sure enough, there it was on the 6 o'clock news…

Announcer: "Three men of Native American descent are wanted for assault and battery on five men, and $10,000's worth of damage to the Malamute Bar in the Old First Ward. Two of the five men suffered severe injuries and one man who was thrown over the bar has a broken arm. It is believed the three are from the Six Nations Seneca Reservation in Irving. Arrest warrants will be issued as soon as authorities are able to establish their identity. In defense of the three in question, a few witnesses stated that the five men who suffered injuries had harassed the three Senecas.

Before the fight actually started, one of the five white men was quoted as saying something to the effect…, 'We don't want you Indians in here! Why don't you go back to the reservation and do a rain dance!' Channel 2 will follow up on this story and report any new development as it becomes available."

Hawk had been on the wrong side of the law before. As a teen, he was brought in for petty theft and another time, for breaking and entering. In court, the charges amounted to misdemeanors. Beyond that, his record had been clean, especially after getting married and fathering a child. He settled down to a quiet life, working every day and being responsible.

Now what?! He was probably looking at jail time for what happened. He really feared going to jail. A good friend told him that he should leave town and get lost somewhere until things blow over. He had become a good family man and didn't want to leave them. He was torn but knew that if he didn't leave, things could get really bad for him and his family. It killed him having to do this.

He had to break the news to his son. He sat him down and said, "Jacob, something bad happened and daddy has to go away for awhile. I won't be around to take care of you and mom and need you to help take care of things till I get back. I promise I will call often. You need to promise me you'll listen to mom, go to school every day and do well. You'll need to do your homework and your chores. I'm counting on you to not let me down, okay?"

With great big tears in his eyes, Jacob said, "Daddy, I don't want you go! You've gone away to work so many times. Every time you go, I'm really, really sad! I cry a lot, daddy. Please don't go!"

Hawk wrapped his arms around his boy, held him tight and said, "You trust dad, right? Then trust me when I say I'll be back as soon as I can. And when I do, I'll find a way to never have to go away again. Okay?" He held him tight for a while until he felt he could leave. He then kissed his cheek and said, "Remember, I'll be back as soon as I can. I love you Jake!"

He also had a talk with Diana and assured her that he'd be back as soon as possible. She had to endure him being gone for several weeks before, for out-of-town jobs, but this was going to be way different. Neither she nor Hawk knew when he'd be back. They could only hope it wouldn't be very long.

His people gathered up money for him and the other two so they could leave town. It wasn't much, but enough for them to get out of town, and get somewhere where they could find work. The three men said their good-byes and left. One went to Rochester, one to Syracuse, and Hawk headed for the north end of Manhattan in New York City.

For a little over four months now, Hawk has been doing the best he could to stay under the radar. He keeps in touch with his family on a weekly basis at set times so they won't miss each other. This is done through friends who receive his calls and in turn, signal his wife Diana to come over to their house and speak to him. It's done this way in case there should be a tap on her phone. If someone calls the house and her line happens to be tapped by the cops, they'll only hear friends and family calling, not Hawk.

He told Diana that he planned on making his way back home as soon as he got the okay from people close to the case. A lawyer for the reservation was trying to work things out with the courts, police and the bar owner. Right now, it's a wait-and-see situation. He's hoping things will get resolved soon. He was glad the bartender, a couple of the patrons and the hippy made official statements that the five men were the cause of the fight. But still, there were damages to pay, and an arrest warrant was issued for him and his friends.

While hiding in New York City's Marcus Garvey Park area, he does whatever jobs he can get to gather money that will pay for the damages to the bar, to square things with the owner.

As for the charges, he's been told that they should be dropped soon. The case was brought before a judge who has received depositions from the witnesses stating that Hawk and his friends were attacked and acted in self-defense.

He's so looking forward to going back home and be with his family and friends. He misses them a lot. His heart breaks every time he thinks about his son and wife at home, without him. For now, he has to wait for something good to happen. This is taking an awful toll on him.

CHAPTER 5

VAGRANT NUMBER TWO

The north side cops have their bum and the south side is just about to pick up theirs. Captain Durso has a meeting with officers Abe Percy and Terry Duffy. Percy is black and Duffy, white Irish…of course. Both men are in their mid-thirties.

They get the same directions from their captain as the north side team got concerning their task of picking up a vagrant. Unlike Weber and Perez, Percy and Duffy don't care who they pick up. To them, it's a stupid assignment. They don't like picking on bums, as they call them, and would rather be busting dope pushers, murderers or pimps. But when their captain says, "Get!" they get going in doing whatever he says. It is part respect for his rank and part fear of retribution if they go against his orders.

The captain is all about…"respect and honor for the department." He's known for exercising the law, pretty much, "by the book." And, he's big on having his officers handle things on the streets in a professional manner.

As Officer Percy is driving the squad car at 8:30 pm on Fulton Street near Saint Paul's Chapel, Duffy reaches the point when he's had enough of searching for a bum they can pull in. He tells his partner to pull over. The car stops, Duffy gets out, looks around the crowd on the sidewalk for an unsuspecting vagrant. About ten paces away, he sees his target.

He walks up to him and asks, "What's your name?"

"George," he says. "What do you want from me?"

Duffy looks at his partner in the squad car. Percy sticks his head out of the window and yells, "Yeah, that's him! He fits the description of the man we're looking for."

Duffy turns George around and slaps his handcuffs on him!

George yells, "Hey! What are you doing?!"

"Are you resisting?!" says Duffy.

"I didn't do nothing, man! Of course I'm resisting! You can't just put me in cuffs! What did I do?"

Duffy looks back at Percy in the squad car, winks at him and tells George, "You just admitted to me that you resisted. That's what you did! So…. you're coming with me."

George is peeved and yells, "You gotta be kidding me, man!"

"No, I'm not kidding!" says Duffy. "And stop calling me, MAN! You're going for a ride to the station. Don't say another word or I'll add 'unruly conduct' to the first charge."

George gives him a dirty look and says, "Unruly conduct!!! This stinks! This STINKS! …BIG TIME!"

As Duffy leads him to the car, Percy is waiting with the back door open. He pats him down and has him sit in the back of the cruiser. They head for the precinct house to deposit their catch.

While heading for the station, Percy says. "George is your name huh? George what?"

"Just George! I go by George. Everybody just knows me by George. Is that a problem?"

"Not a problem Georgie. I like the name. Only, you gotta come up with your whole name. You gotta know I can't process you at the station with just the name, George. What's your full, real name?"

He sighs and says, "George Freeman... George Henry Freeman."

Treating him like a half-whit, Percy says, "See now! That wasn't so hard was it George Henry Freeman?"

Again, he asks why he was arrested. Duffy plays with his mind a bit and says, "Who said you were under arrest?"

"You did, man!"

"You need to pay attention Georgie! I never said you were under arrest. I said... you resisted me. And there you go with the 'MAN' thing again!"

"If I'm not under arrest, then why am I in these cuffs and in this car?"

Duffy says, "Just because."

"Just because," George says in a mocking tone.

Duffy tells him, "That's right! Just because."

Very irritated, George snaps back, "Just because of what?!"

Both Percy and Duffy respond in unison –"JUST BECAUSE!!!"

He sits back and mumbles to himself, "Because, because, because they're STUPID! That's what it is!"

Percy says, "I heard that George Henry! Just SHUT UP and sit there quiet like, okay?! We're almost at the station."

All the while the three are making their way through the traffic, both officers spot several bad drivers committing traffic infractions, one guy even runs a red light right in front of them.

Percy breaks the silence and says, "You know, we just arrested a bum for no good reason instead of stopping some of these idiots who might run over somebody."

With that said, George pipes in, "That's right! Why not let me go and you two can go and arrest some of those bad drivers?! And by the way, I'M NOT A BUM! I've been through a string of very bad things that put me on the streets."

"Oh no Georgie, we couldn't let you go out there among those bad drivers." says Duffy. "Heck, they might run you over! See how we're doing you a favor by taking you off the streets?"

George answers them, "Not me! I'd stay out of traffic. I promise!"

"Forget it," says Duffy. "We're going to make real sure you're safe for the night." Feeling a bit bad for the way he treated him, he adds, "Sorry about the bad stuff that put you on the streets pal. And, accept my apology for calling you a bum. You're not a bum, you're a fine gentleman."

George thanks him, but in his mind, he flashes back to the reason he became a street person and sinks back into the seat in a depressed mood. He so wishes his situation was different. He truly wants to get a normal life. For now, this is the reality of his existence. He's come to accept that and prays daily that things will get better for him.

They finally arrive at the south precinct and deposit their passenger in a cell for a good night's sleep. Part of the instructions for both teams of officers was to contact their captains when they had their man at the station house… in a cell by themselves. They were not to be mixed in with other individuals who were brought in. That part of the instructions also confused all of the officers, from both the north and south stations. They wondered, why a separate cell from the other prisoners. This added to their bewilderment about the assignment.

After performing their duties, Percy and Duffy get back to patrolling the streets. What puzzles the officers from both precincts is that none of them know what the actual reason was for the strange assignment. None of them ever had anything like that happen before. There was something really odd about it and the thought of it didn't leave them. They figured they'd eventually be given a reason. Part of their thinking is, "The guys in charge do weird things on occasion."

To answer the question "why" they get such a stupid assignments from time to time, the officers at their station have come up with a little song using a famous quote from Alfred Lord Tennyson. They do a little ditty with it…"Ours is not to reason why, ours is but to do and die. …ours is not to reason why, ours is but to do and die." They laugh about it and go do what they are told to do.

CHAPTER 6

GEORGE'S BACKGROUND

George is a native New Yorker who has hit a few bumps in life. He dropped out of high school in his second year and had several other jobs before having the opportunity of learning carpentry as a trade. That was a very good thing for a dropout. He learned well and thought that's what he was going to do for the rest of his working days. Unfortunately, after a little over a year and a half, work slowed right down and he was laid off. He was devastated. But as fate would have it, he ran into a friend who got him a job at a food processing plant where he became a line foreman and had been making decent money. This was excellent for a man with no real skills and not much education.

He was married to a woman named Jenny who was a bit hard to get along with at times, but he made the marriage work for the sake of their only child, eight year old, Beau. His name means "handsome" in French. That boy was his world. His son was the reason he got up each day and went to work. And, when he came home, he couldn't wait to spend time with his boy. He loved talking to him, playing games or going for bike rides.

He had a good paying job, (money in his pocket), a nice house in a great neighborhood, and neighbors, Denny and Jane as best friends. He felt that he had all he could need for the moment. Life was good.

TRAGEDY STRIKES

Sometimes, life has a way of taking a man as low as he can possibly go. One day while waiting in front of the house to greet his boy where the school bus dropped him off, the unimaginable happened! As always, the bus stopped on the opposite side of the street with its flashing red lights on and the stop sign extended out. This day, some idiot raced by and hit Beau after he passed in front of the bus as he made his way to cross the street. He was sent tumbling a hundred feet across his own front lawn. George saw it all and was sent into immediate psychological and emotional shock. Right at that moment, his world came crashing down and his heart was shattered. His boy was everything to him. He couldn't accept losing him that way. Beau died from massive body and head injuries. The sight of his little boy's mutilated body on the front lawn was etched in his mind. He would never be the same. He just couldn't overcome the pain of that loss.

The driver had neither license nor insurance. He'd lost his license due to DWI infractions. He was sent to prison for a term of seven to fifteen years, but George and Jenny now had a lifetime of pain to endure. They were completely devastated!

At the funeral, George wept uncontrollably. They both took a long time to grieve. Jenny went through a good year of grieving before she could get back to as normal a life as possible. George's situation went way beyond that. He fell into a deep depression and began drinking heavily. Liquor became a major part of his life and only added to his miseries.

He was thirty-two years old when he got hooked on booze. His life started unraveling and it took him to a point of no return. In time, he found himself in deep trouble! He lost his job, and… to add insult to injury, he found out his wife was having an affair with their good neighbor, Denny. Part of the reason for that was his boozing. He was out in bars more than home, trying to drown the pain of losing Beau. Jenny came to lean on Denny for consolation and affection. George didn't blame her. In his state of mind, he just couldn't be there for her.

He divorced, lost the house and ran out of whatever money he had after paying off his wife in the divorce settlement. Being jobless, penniless, and homeless, booze became his only friend and rendered him unable to function as a normal working man. Life had beaten him down. Now, he was on the streets with countless other miserable people who, for one reason or another, became "bums." Having nothing and no one, he came to rely on an organization called The Neighborhood Coalition for shelter, food and socializing.

An Awakening

After several months on the streets of South Manhattan, one day while sitting across from a church with a bagged whisky bottle in his hand, he looked up at the cross on the steeple and stared at a cloud in the sky above it. He could swear he saw his boy's face appear.

He thought to himself, *"Beau is watching me. My boy is watching me!"*

Just then, he was cut to the heart, realizing that if his boy could actually see what he had become, he wouldn't be very proud of him; he'd be ashamed. That hit him hard, very hard! It struck a major chord in his heart. He broke down and began weeping.

He looked up at that cloud with tears in his eyes and said, "Beau, I miss you so much! My heart is still broken and I can't get over losing you, son. I know I'm a mess right now and you don't want dad to be like this. I promise that I will do what I need to do to make you proud of me. You are always in my heart and on my mind. Oh…how I miss you! I love you so very much. Keep me in your sights from above and guide me as I work to get out of this miserable life I've allowed myself to get into. Starting today, I will clean myself up, I promise! I love you so much Beau, and miss you!"

He sat there weeping for a good while as he thought about the loss of his son and the poor condition he allowed himself to sink to. After some time of evaluating his situation, he made up his mind he was going to fix his broken life. He knew it would be hard, but he was determined to start right away.

He stopped drinking and focused on doing the best he could to survive and keep his promise to his son. Every morning, he woke up with Beau on his mind. It kept him on the right track. He volunteered at a homeless shelter that provided him with a room and meals. The director would hand him $50 a week for his work in hopes that he'd go out and look for work. He'd been doing that now for the past three months and kept at it every day.

One thing unique about George Henry Freeman was that he always liked looking neat by wearing decent clothes. As a line foreman, he was used to wearing shirts and ties. He didn't like looking sloppy and this aspect of his persona followed him into the life he was now living.

After his talk with Beau, he kept himself well-shaved most of the time and managed to get good-looking clothes at the Goodwill Store so as to present himself on the streets as a man still having pride and self-respect. His favorite coat was a London Fog, one of the things he still had from when he was married. It made him look classier than the rest of the homeless. It was worth about $150. He kept it locked up at the mission while he hung out on the streets and mingled with other homeless men. He'd wear it when looking for work. He wore a worn out aviator coat as his everyday coat that he got from the Goodwill store for $15 shortly after making the streets his home.

He's a five foot ten, handsome and intelligent guy. This life on the street is not for him. After having had that little chat with Beau, he really wanted to become a respectable man again. His days were now spent looking for a steady job, any fair paying job. All he needed was the right break. He's also a religious man and prays for God to create some sort of miracle for him.

Chapter 7

George's release

After an okay night's sleep, George is brought out of his cell at noon and is found standing in front of the officer who will process him out. He's still very confused about the whole thing. He was dragged into precinct jailhouses before when he was drunk, but this time, it was just weird! The last time he spent the night in a cell was when a kindhearted cop found him sleeping outside in the freezing cold and called for a squad car so he wouldn't freeze to death, but this time, it was just strange.

Before leaving the station, our man wanted some answers. He had a tendency of being a little pushy, an "in your face" kind of guy.

He walks over to the front desk and says to the sergeant, his name is Sergeant Thomas, "Can you tell me why the hell I was brought in here last night, and now, you release me, just like that?"

The sergeant looks at him with a frown on his face and tells him, "I don't know why. I didn't ask why. I don't care why! I just did as I was told to do by the captain; to let you go by noon today. It's noon! So...I'm letting you go. Now, go away and let me work!"

George says out loud, "This is nuts! You guys are nuts!"

A bit irritated, the sergeant says, "Just go away Georgie! Okay?"

"Okay! Okay boss! Uh, you got five dollars you can loan me for a sandwich and a coffee?"

"And you'd pay me back, right? Yeah right! Get the hell out of here Mr. Freeman! You're beginning to really irritate me! That's not good! You want something to eat, go to a mission house. SCRAM! ....NOW!"

He walks out of the precinct, takes to the sidewalk and heads toward the mission house where he can get food and attend to his duties there.

CHAPTER 8

Hawk's release

Meanwhile at the north precinct, like George, Hawk is brought out from his cell to the front desk at noon to be released. Sergeant Hicks is on duty. The officer gives him his few belongings and tells him that he's free to go. He's confused and wants to know what the heck that was all about, getting picked up, put in a cell for the night and released?

The sergeant tells him, "We just wanted to keep you safe for the night."

"Keep me safe for the night from what?" says Hawk.

"From all of the terrible people who could have hurt you out there on the bad streets of New York. You know it's dangerous out there Hawk. Now take yourself out of here. Have a nice day."

Hawk looks at him with a bit of a scowl on his face and leaves before he says something that might really get him into trouble.

THE MESSENGER

As soon as he steps out the precinct door, one of Mr. Blanchard's messengers walks up to him and asks if he'd like to receive a large sum of money – for free?

He's caught off guard by such a statement, laughs at the man and says, "Yeah right! You're going to give me a lot of money, for free? Why? What do I have to do to get it? And…how much money are you talking about?"

The messenger asks him to get in the limo so he can explain everything. He tells him, "There's no catch, I assure you. You were chosen to take part in an experiment that will absolutely give you a small fortune. Are you willing to hear me out? You can walk away if you think this is not for real or a scam. We can easily get someone else to get this very generous sum of money."

He stands back and processes the offer, *It's kind of weird that I just came out of the police station and this guy dressed in a suit offers me a bunch of money. What the hell. What have I got to lose? I got nothin' better to do.*

He looks at the messenger straight in the eyes and with a stern look, he says, "Okay! I'll hear you out, but this better not be a joke! I don't like to be made a fool of!"

"I understand." says the messenger. "I assure you you'll want to do this once you hear all the details."

Hawk gets in the limo and the driver is told to go to the north side of Manhattan, to Mount Morris Park.

Wanting to get a feel to see if Hawk would be a good candidate for this large monetary gift, he asks him, "What would you do if you had a lot of money right now?"

Hawk folds his arms, then puts his left hand to his chin, thinks for a moment and says, "Man, I would get back to my wife and son in Buffalo and be with my people again. I would square away a problem I had there and get back to a normal life. That's what I'd do if I had a lot of money"

His host tells him that if he's willing to follow the directions in the envelope he's holding, he can very well make that happen. Hawk is really curious and wants to know exactly what he'll need to do.

He says to the man, "Okay! I'm game. Tell me what I have to do. I need to get back home. I'm dying in this damn city. I don't belong here!"

"I understand your feelings about this city," says the messenger. "It sure is a big city …and very difficult for outsiders to get used to. I believe what I'm about to offer you will help your situation in a big way."

He gives him an envelope and is told that he cannot open it until he's dropped off. With that, he is handed a chain with a medal of Saint Christopher and a baseball cap with the New Orleans Saints' emblem on it.

The messenger tells him, "Put the medal around your neck and wear the cap. It is 'extremely important' that you do not remove them. Once we drop you off, you must read the instructions very carefully! If all goes well, you should be able to complete the assignment in the time stated on the instruction sheet, then, go and enjoy your good fortune. Good luck my friend!"

The limo reaches its destination. Hawk puts the medal around his neck, the cap on his head and exits the car with the envelope firmly in his hand. He's dropped off at 124th and Madison where Blanchard's shadows, Joe and Fritz, are waiting to do what they were hired to do; follow their man and provide video to the CREW.

He watches the limo pull away and looks around to find a spot where he can open the envelope to see what's inside. He finds an alley where he can have some privacy. Once he feels secluded enough, he quickly tears the flap off the envelope and takes out its contents. He sees the check in the plastic sleeve and reads what he can. It's only the right side of it and all he can read is, *"thousand dollars and 00/100 cents."*

He's stumped! He can't figure out how much money this represents. He only sees half a check.

He says to himself, "If it's a thousand dollars, that's not really a lot of money." He takes out the instruction sheet and begins reading...

YOU HAVE HALF OF A CASHIER'S CHECK IN THE AMOUNT OF $200,000 DOLLARS. $100,000 IS FOR YOU AND $100,000 IS FOR ANOTHER MAN BY THE NAME OF GEORGE, WHO HAS THE OTHER HALF. YOU WILL MAKE YOUR WAY TO THE TIMES SQUARE AND PEDESTRIAN MALL AREA TO BEGIN LOOKING FOR EACH OTHER STARTING EARLY TOMORROW MORN-

ing. George will also be wearing a black New Orleans Saints baseball cap. It will have a "Fleur-de-lis" on it. That's the Saints' team logo. You can verify who you are by showing each other your Saint Christopher medal. You will have until 3 PM tomorrow to find each other. Then, both of you will go to the Businessmen's Finance Bank on 9th Avenue and 20th Street in the Chelsea District. Once there, you will speak to bank manager Dexter Druitt who will combine the two halves of the check. He will have both of you sign it and give each of you $100,000. God's speed! Very important, TRUST NO ONE!

Hawk smiles real big thinking that he might actually get $100,000 dollars. He reads the instructions again and takes a look at the half check one more time. He then puts the two items back in the manila envelope, folds it carefully and tucks it in a large inside pocket of his wool navy pea coat. He puts his left hand on his chest to find the Saint Christopher medal, squeezes it and says, "Okay Saint Christopher, lead the way!"

He starts making his way toward Times Square by walking west on 124th. When he reaches Fifth Avenue, he'll need to go south. That'll take him to the Square. The whole trek will be over seventy blocks long. As he makes his way, he wonders how many people are going to be in the Square and how he's going to go about zeroing in on this guy named George! For now, he just plans on getting there and figures he'll think of something once he arrives.

Shadows Joe and Fritz are following him on foot and send video via their cell phones to "the Crew," (Blanchard, Malich and Gage). This way, they're able to see in real time what their man is doing.

Hawk has no idea that when he hid himself from onlookers to open his envelope, Blanchard's men got a video of him doing so. Blanchard and his men are happy that he read the directions and knows what to do. The shadows stay with him as he heads towards his destination to find his "check partner," George.

CHAPTER 9

GEORGE AND THE MESSENGER

When George was released from the south police station, his plan was to go to the homeless shelter where he stays. As he's making his way there, Blanchard's messenger has the limo driver stop a short distance ahead of him.

He gets out of the car, walks over toward him and says, "Excuse me, sir. You've been chosen to receive a sum of money; a very large sum. Will you come inside the limousine so I can explain in more details?"

George looks at him and says, "Are you putting me on, man?!"

"No sir, I assure you this is for real. Please get in and I'll explain."

He's really suspicious. The messenger is standing by the open limo door and motions for him to get in.

George says, "Is this some kind of joke? If it is, I'll punch your lights out, man! I'm not in the mood to be involved in some scam you're trying to run on me!"

"Sir, I promise you this is no joke, and certainly, not a scam. You've been chosen to receive a large sum of money. Trust me. You won't regret it."

Still very skeptical, he walks to the car and gets in. The messenger tells him that he will be driven to the southern end of Manhattan and that he'll receive specific instructions that he will need to follow.

As they ride along, the messenger asks George what he would do if he had a lot of money. He hopes to get a good response. The "Crew" wants the money to go to men who won't waste it.

Well, George doesn't let them down. He tells his host, "Wow man! I've lost everything! I have nothing. If I had a good chunk of money, I'd get cleaned up and get myself productive again. I don't belong on the streets. I'm smart and have skills. I hate being out here! I would absolutely get myself right again and never return to this kind of life. As a matter of fact, I recently promised my dead son that I'd do all I can to fix my life."

With that, the messenger nods and tells him that his answer meets with his approval to be the recipient of enough money to restart his life.

The driver gets to the north end of Battery Park and stops. His host takes a manila envelope out of his briefcase and says to him, "This is for you. You are to read the instructions very carefully. Like I stated before, this isn't a scam or joke. The money will be yours. All you need to do is follow the instructions. And…you must wear this Saint Christopher medal around your neck and this Saints hat. They will serve as identification for you to verify that you are the person who is to receive the money. Guard them well. I must stress, it is absolutely essential that you wear both at all times. You'll understand better after you read the instructions. Do you understand all that I've told you?"

George says, "Yeah, yeah, I understand! But, how do I get the money? Is it in the envelope?"

"Just read the instructions," says the messenger. "Everything you need is in there. Good luck to you!"

He's dropped off at the north end of Battery Park near the U.S. Custom House. And like Hawk, he too has shadows tailing him. They are Everett and Hutch. Their job will be to keep George in their sights at all times; to provide the Crew video of anything interesting that he does and to make sure he's safe.

Standing at the edge of the park, there are people all around him. He needs to go somewhere private. He looks at the envelope, tucks it inside his shirt and holds onto to it with both arms wrapped around the front of him. He heads down the avenue looking for a place where he can check out what's inside the package he's been given. The shadows are doing a good job sending the Crew great video feeds. So far, they're very pleased with the way things are going.

It is 1 pm. George is walking down Lower Broadway on the south side of Manhattan. There are quite a few people around and he needs to go where he'll be completely alone. He looks for a secluded spot, ducks into an alley and quickly opens the 5x10 envelope, hoping to find money. He doesn't see any, only a light yellow sheet and a plastic sleeve with a check in it…half a check. He pulls it out and all he can read is, *"Pay to the bearers two hundred…"* He's dumbfounded and doesn't know what to make of it.

When he took out the contents from the envelope, the shadows noticed the instruction sheet slip his grip as he hurried to look at the check. It fell to the ground and blew down the alley and across the street. As they keep an eye on where it's going, Hutch notifies the bosses to tell them what just happened. Everett sends a live feed showing where the sheet landed.

Jacques radios the men and says, *"Maudit"!* (Damn!) No one expected anything like that to happen! WOW! Okay. Just keep an eye on the sheet, and him! We'll see what he does. If he can't find it, we'll intercede. I believe he'll realize very soon that he doesn't have it. Stay vigilant! *Ah oui, très intéressant!* …This should be interesting"

George stares at the check and says to himself, "That's all there is?!" He's really confused, *Two hundred…what? Two hundred dollars! That's it!!! The man said it'd be 'a lot of money.' That's not a lot of money. This must be a joke, man! I knew this was too good to be true! Two hundred dollars! I could beg that in one day if I really hustled!*

He's really upset! More than upset… he's fuming! Then, he remembers the words of the messenger…"Read the instructions!"

He says to himself in a low, but extremely anxious voice, "Instructions, instructions! Oh no! I saw the sheet fall to the ground. Where is it?! Where the hell is it?! Oh NO! I gotta find it!"

On an 18 inch screen in their high tech van, the Crew can see everything that's going on. Everyone is anxious to see how their subject will react to and deal with the situation at hand. They watch and wait.

George puts the check back into the envelope and tucks it inside his shirt, buttons it up and looks for the instruction sheet. There are a lot of papers on the ground. His sheet got mixed up with the rest of the trash blowing around in the alleyway; it's a very windy day. He's beside himself! He doesn't know which way the wind could've taken it.

He cries out, "God help me!!! Please let me find it! I need to find it! Help me please....GOD! OH GOD! PLEASE!"

His heart is in his throat and his eyes well up. The sheet will be hard to find among the other trash he sees blowing around. All he knows is that it's a light yellowish color, nearly white. He starts picking up all the papers around him that even look a little bit yellow, but no luck.

People are looking at him and thinking, *"He must be nuts! Look at him picking up paper and throwing them back down. What could he be looking for?"*

He's frantic, *Could it be for two hundred thousand dollars? GOD, please let me find it!!!*

The very thought that he won't, makes him go nuts! He keeps looking. He screams in his mind! "IT HAS TO BE HERE, BUT WHERE?!"

He looks for a good ten minutes then falls into deep despair. He sits on the ground with his back against a building and just dies inside. His head is down and he feels completely undone. He sits there for a while in total misery, then thinks about retracing his steps. He figures where he opened the envelope and where the sheet fell out. He goes to that spot and tests the wind direction by picking up a piece of paper, letting it drop to the ground and following it as the wind blows it away from him.

He scans the area very carefully. "So much trash," he says to himself. All of a sudden, he stops cold and gasps! His heart almost stops! Lo and behold, he sees a yellow paper about the size of the one he pulled out of the envelope. His mind explodes with excitement! His heart is beating out of his chest as he keeps his gaze on that paper. He says, "That HAS to be it across the street by that bench! God, please let that be it, PLEASE!"

The wind is still blowing it around. He walks hurriedly to the other side of the street and sees that there are several people near the bench and a couple sitting on it. He rushes over and bumps an old man off balance as he dives on top of it, just as a gust of wind begins moving it again. He grabs it firmly and gets up.

Just then, a cop that was about ten feet away and saw all the action, walks over and grabs him by the nape of the neck and yells… "WHAT THE HELL ARE YOU DOING?! You almost knocked that gentleman to the ground! Are you drunk, stoned or out of your mind, fella?"

George says, "I'm not drunk or stoned, officer. I just tripped on the sidewalk. I'm sorry! I'm sorry! Can I go?"

With a hand gesture, the officer motions for him to move along. He has the sheet crumpled in his hand and holds on tight. He feared the cop might ask him what he's holding, but today is his lucky day; the cop doesn't give it any thought. He walks away and says to himself… "Thank you Lord!"

While this happened, the Crew was parked nearby and received all the action via Hutch's cell phone. They're all so relieved that George was able to figure things out. If he hadn't been able to retrieve that instruction sheet, the men would've had to come up with something real quick to fix the problem. In his planning, Jacques hadn't anticipated anything like this. Now that all is well, on with the surveillance!

With the instructions in hand, George gets away from the crowd and finds another alley where he can be completely alone and out of sight. He straightens out the sheet and begins reading it…

You have half of a cashier's check in the amount of $200,000 dollars. $100,000 is for you and $100,000 is for another man by the name of Hawk who has the other half. You will make your way to the Times Square and Pedestrian Mall area to begin looking for each other starting early tomorrow morning. Hawk will also be wearing a black New Orleans Saints baseball cap. It will have a "Fleur-de-lis" on it. That's the Saints' team logo. You can verify who you are by showing each other your Saint Christopher medal. You will have until 3 pm tomorrow to find each other. Then, both of you will go to the Businessmen's Finance Bank on 9th Avenue and 20th Street in the Chelsea District. Once there, you will speak

TO BANK MANAGER DEXTER DRUITT WHO WILL COMBINE THE TWO HALVES OF THE CHECK. HE WILL HAVE BOTH OF YOU SIGN IT AND GIVE EACH OF YOU $100,000. GOD'S SPEED! VERY IMPORTANT, TRUST NO ONE!

He's beyond excited! He's deliriously happy and can hardly contain himself. He wants to scream with joy…but doesn't want to attract attention. He gets back to the sidewalk, walks a bit and stops in an indented doorway of a closed store; faces the door and takes out the check to look at it again.

He feels like this is all a dream, and thinks, *It doesn't make sense! Why would anybody give me a $100,000?*

He doesn't know who the benefactor is, but figures he's going for it. He reasons, "What do I have to lose? I have nothing now and if this is for real, then I'm gonna be $100,000 richer!"

He makes sure the instruction sheet and the half check are very secure in the envelope. He tucks it inside his shirt just above his belt and completely buttons up his coat. Then, he says out loud, "Okay feet, let's get moving! I gotta find this guy Hawk!"

CHAPTER 10

KEEPING THE CHECK SAFE

Having all the information; who to look for, the location for the contact person and what bank to go to, George is a bit anxious. The first thing that worries him is how he'll find Hawk in the Times Square, Pedestrian Mall area with maybe hundreds or thousands of people there. His mind is reeling, but he knows that he's got to make it happen. The thought of having $100,000 in his hands spurs him on.

Since he has spent some time on the streets, he's well aware that some of the vagrants out there would cut someone's throat for a good pair of shoes or sneakers. If anyone found out what he's hiding under his shirt, he'd be more than a major target. He's sure that he'll be able to keep his prize well hidden. But, his concern is Hawk; what to do once he finds him, and how should he approach him to make the deal happen without any problems?

He continues to roll all of that in his mind and realizes that he cannot have the half check on him when they connect. The messenger's warning about "not trusting anyone" rings in his head. He doesn't know what this guy Hawk might do. He thinks to himself, *There are no names on the check, just... 'Pay to the bearers...' What if he has a friend, and they band together to take my half of the money?*

That thought scares him! He wonders what he can do to make sure nothing weird like that happens. As he puts more thought into it, he finally comes up with a solution.

He says to himself, "Before I go to Times Square, I'll go and hide my part of the check somewhere near the bank. That way, when Hawk and I meet, I'll have a bit of time to feel him out and see what kind of guy he is. If everything looks good, we'll make our way to put those two check halves together; I'll get my half where I've hidden it, walk in the bank and get our money. Big question! Where do I put it?"

The problem right now is that he's quite a bit south of the bank. He figures he'll take the subway to get to 9th and 20th where the bank is located. Once there, he can scout out the area and figure out where he can hide his check, then make his way to Times Square by four or five o'clock.

Even though the search for Hawk is to start the following morning, he hopes that maybe his "check buddy" will also be in the area and will spot him as he has a look around later today or tonight. He plans on doing that until it's time to find a place to sleep. He realizes that it's a long shot, but one that's worth a try.

At the moment, he has no idea Hawk is on the north end of Manhattan and that he also has many blocks to travel before getting to Times Square. He too, has the idea of looking for George as soon as he gets there today.

Now at the subway entrance, George goes down and hops on a northbound train that will take him near the bank. There are quite a few stops along the way and it takes him a fair amount of time getting there. After a few more stops, he's finally at his destination.

He feels confident walking around, having retrieved his London Fog coat from the homeless shelter before setting out. He doesn't look too shabby. Wearing it should give people the impression that he's some kind of businessman.

As he nears the bank and looks around for an ideal place to stash his half of the check, he can't seem to come up with the right place to do that. He's about to give up on the idea, when suddenly, he sees the bank and says to himself, "That's where I'll put it…right inside the bank!"

It's a quarter to two and the bank is very busy. It's perfect for what he needs to do. He looks around to scope things out for a few moments and sees there are slips for deposits and withdrawals at each customer counter and…tape dispensers.

He takes the envelope from inside his shirt, goes to a teller's window and asks in a very professional tone, "Could I please have five of your bank envelopes for night deposits? My business closes after bank hours and I will need to make night deposits."

He's given the envelopes and walks over to one of the counters, one that is the most secluded, and is perhaps, out of range of the bank cameras. He places himself at the end of the counter near the wall. This positioning is important because it will allow him to do what he has in mind to do; put his half of the check in a bank envelope and stick it on the back of the counter next to the wall.

He pretends he's filling out one of the forms and puts it in an envelope, then seals it with the tape. He fills out a second form and puts his half check in another envelope and sticks a sufficient amount of tape to it so that he's sure it will adhere well behind the customer counter. In case there's a camera viewing his actions, he does a bit of a "misdirection" move. He has a few deposit slips on the counter, nudges them with his elbow and knocks them to the floor. As he bends over to pick them up, his left hand secretly attaches the taped envelope to the back of the counter that only has a three inch gap between it and the wall. He's very confident the large counter will not be moved since it's made of marble and weighs at least five hundred pounds. With that done, he feels much better knowing his half of the check will be safe.

Before leaving the bank, he notices a name plate on a private office door. It belongs to the man he and Hawk will need to talk to once they pair up and come in to get their money. It's Dexter Druitt's office. There's a window in the door. As he walks over nonchalantly to look inside in order to get a better peek at him, he notices that he's talking to a police officer. He can see two silver bars on the cop's uniform and knows he's a captain. After getting a good look at Druitt and the officer, he leaves the bank to catch a subway to get to Times Square. It's a little past two thirty.

TROUBLE DOWN BELOW

While waiting at the underground platform for a train, a couple of young punks with a knife corner him and demand he turn over any money he has. Well, as it turns out, our former foreman made it a habit of carrying a "decoy wallet" with fake bills in it. As you look at it folded, all you see is what appears to be paper money in the bills section. He makes like he's afraid and cowers like a puppy and hands over the wallet. One of the robbers looks at it in its folded form and sees what appears to be a lot of money. He's sure he's got a good score. He nudges his cohort and off they go, up the stairs and onto the streets. In the meantime, George's train comes in. He gets on and rides away, smiling. As noted before, he's smart!

The two thieves can't wait to see how much money they got. They duck behind a building, take out the wallet to see how well they did. As the one who took it pulls out the bills, both men soon find out they've been outsmarted. There's a note along with the fake bills.

It says, *"Sorry to ruin your day, but you got exactly what you deserve. As the Bible says, 'The love of money is the root of all evil.' You robbed someone who is down on his luck... Shame on you! Enjoy the fake bills!"*

George's shadows didn't interfere. They were ready to move in only if it looked like he was going to be hurt or if they got the envelope containing the check and instruction sheet.

If the thieves had gotten that, one of the shadows was ready to jump in as a stranger helping a victim. George wouldn't have known he was being helped by someone in the Crew's entourage. Shadow Hutch fed the Crew cell phone video of the entire episode. Everyone is very relieved that it didn't turn out to be a serious situation.

Jacques comments on the outcome through their two-way system, "As I said before men, anything can happen. I'm glad you guardian angels didn't have to get directly involved. Thanks for being there guys. Stay close to him."

Shadow Everett clicks in and says, "Roger that boss! We'll keep Georgie safe, over and out."

CHAPTER 11

HAWK'S BUS RIDE

As George rides toward Times Square after his visit to the bank and the robbery, Hawk is topside on a city bus, heading to the same place. One of his shadows, Fritz, is onboard and the other, Joe, is following in a van.

George is a New Yorker and is used to riding subways, but Hawk doesn't like riding below ground inside those cars with a bunch of people pressing against him. He likes his space. Even riding buses bothers him. He's seen too many ignorant, misbehaved, and stupid people the few times he's ridden them, especially teenagers. To him, they lack common sense, common courtesy and respect for people in general. He views most of them as, "stupid kids!" He has zero tolerance for their delinquent behavior.

Wouldn't you know it, as the bus makes its way toward Times Square, Hawk hears some young moron bad-mouthing an elderly lady. This sends him into a mild rage.

He screams in his mind, *"Në:gëh de 'tge:i"* (This ain't right!") He gets up, walks toward the youth who has his back to him, grabs and squeezes his neck with his huge hand. The lad freezes as he feels great pain!

He tells him, "It hurts, huh? How would you like me to snap your neck, punk?! You need to apologize to this lady, and mean it! Who the hell do you think you are talking to this woman like that? How would you like it if I treated YOUR mom that way? Now, apologize!"

He makes a sincere apology, Hawk lets go of his neck, and the kid is quick to get off at the next stop.

Again, Jacques and his men are fed video of the whole thing by Fritz.

Rick from the Crew says, "Man! That boy was lucky Hawk didn't really hurt him!"

As George and Hawk are occupied making their way to Times Square, some of the men in the crew take time to rest a bit. Hawk's other shadow, Joe, is resting in the van.

Everett and Hutch who are following George in the subway have it a little tougher, having to put up with the crowd on board. They'll soon be relieved by two other men.

The bus ride is slow with all the stops it has to make. About a third of the way there Hawk feels a need to relieve himself and gets off the bus. Of course, Fritz gets off as well. He goes into a Dunkin Donut restaurant to do his business.

When he exits the place, a man bumps into him and he feels a touch inside his coat. He grabs the man's arm before he can retract it, turns him around and puts him in a rear choke hold. A cop on patrol nearby sees the commotion and yells at Hawk to let go of him.

Hawk tells him, "I just caught this guy trying to pick my pocket! No! I won't let him go! Arrest him!"

Hawk is super peeved knowing he could have lost his part of the $200,000 check. He really wants to choke the guy!

The policeman approaches the two and says, "Well, well… Midas Touch! Got caught this time, hey? Maybe I should let this BIG fella choke you a little longer or let him break your fingers. How would that be?"

"You know this guy?" says Hawk.

"Oh yeah! He's a regular slight-of-hand artist around here and has been locked up a few times for this." He turns to the thief and says, "Guess it's time for you to go and stay in our luxury jail house again, huh Midas?"

Midas yells! "I didn't do nothin' man! This guy bumped into ME! …and my hand ACCIDENTLY…got caught in his coat! I SWEAR it, man! I swear it!"

The cop says, "Alright Midas, that's enough! I know you and you know me. I've busted you a couple of times myself for you thieving on people." He cuffs him and says, "Now, move it or I'll let this very large gentleman deal with you in a way you wouldn't like!"

He's led away to the nearest precinct to be processed for pickpocketing activity. The Crew got video of all that, sent by shadow Fritz who was hidden in the shadows thirty feet away. They had a good laugh about it, but are relieved Midas didn't snag the valuable package Hawk has in his coat.

As they watch Hawk retake the street, they see him pull out the envelope a bit from inside his coat and then shoving it right back in. He then buttons it up tight to make sure no other guy like Midas can get to his precious fortune.

He stands at the bus stop that's closest to the doughnut shop for his next ride. In case he got a look at Fritz on the first bus and might recognize him if he got on with him, Joe will take over.

The bus arrives and everyone gets on. Joe waits to see where Hawk sits, then goes three seats across the aisle behind him. He has his cell phone on and sends video to the rest of the men showing Hawk reading a newspaper that was on his seat.

Joe can hear Blanchard in his earpiece, "Enjoy the ride, Joe."

He smiles and double clicks his two-way as if to say, "Thanks boss."

The bus has just passed the midpoint of the trek. Hawk keeps looking up at the street signs from time to time to see where he is. He wants to make sure he doesn't miss his stop. Joe can see that his subject is looking a bit nervous. He puts himself in his place and can imagine the many thoughts that are going through his head. Times Square is a fairly large area with tons of people. This may prove to be a bit overwhelming for him. Time will tell.

THE BOSS SPEAKS

Blanchard has an impromptu meeting on the two-way system with all the men involved in the chase. He says, "Hey gentlemen, so far we've had a few unexpected surprises in this pursuit, and our two subjects haven't even connected yet. Tomorrow, when they're both in the Times Square area trying to find each other in a massive crowd, it could prove to be the most hectic part of this adventure. I can't wait to see how they find each other and what will happen after our two subjects get their money from the bank. It's very possible that it won't be the end of our involvement. Who knows what can happen? I wonder what they'll do with the money once it's actually in their hands. Will they take a few hundred with them and set up an account at the bank to make sure the bulk of their fortune is safe or will they take the whole amount with them? If one or both of them take it all, would any of you want to predict what might happen? It should be interesting how this will all unfold.

One more thing, who knows if someone inside, or outside the bank will be watching them. There are crooks out there that scout out banks and zero in on unsuspecting customers who make large cash withdrawals. Some have been robbed right outside the bank while others have been followed and got hit at home.

It could be a while before we rest. We'll need to stay with them till we're sure all is well. It would be a shame if the money fell into the wrong hands. It'll be our job to make sure that doesn't happen. *Merci mes amis* for your good work! Much appreciated!"

Hutch responds: "Hey boss, this is pretty interesting. Personally, I can't wait to see the end of this tale. It'd make a great movie!"

Rick Gage comes back with, "That's a great idea! After this is all over, we should hire a screen writer to work out a script for a movie. What do you think Jacques?"

"A movie?" Jacques replies, "Why not? We've been benefactors, why not movie producers? Okay men, enough dreaming for the moment. We can talk about that later. Right now, let's just keep track of our guys. What's Georgie doing now?"

Everett radios in that they're still with him on the subway and should be arriving at Times Square in about fifteen minutes.

CHAPTER 12

GEORGE'S TREK TO TIMES SQUARE

George's shadows, Everett and Hutch, keep close tabs on their man as they all roll along toward Times Square. They're sitting diagonally across from him, and from time to time, they can see him feeling the envelope under his shirt as a way of making sure that it's still safe and secure.

They smile at each other and Hutch whispers, "Lucky guy! $100,000 just handed to him."

"It's not in his hands yet! How long do you think it's going to last him?" replies Everett. "Usually, people who have nothing and suddenly get a big chunk of dough don't do too well managing it."

Hutch asks, "And, what would you do with that much cash?"
"I'd take a nice long vacation somewhere for about a month then come back home and continue working. That money won't last

forever. It'll only go as long as he can stretch it. Hopefully, he'll be smart with it."

GETTING CLOSE

Our travelers are nearing Times Square. It's a little after four-thirty in the afternoon when the rail car rolls to a stop and everyone gets off. The shadows break off so that one is behind about ten steps, and the other stays fairly close to him, but always well hidden. This is crucial in case something unexpected happens and there's a need for them to act fast. They're about to get mixed in with a whole bunch of people.

George heads up the stairs to street level. Right away, he's hit with the fact that it's mobbed. He gets his bearings and sees Times Square off to his left. He makes his way there in order to walk through the Square and Pedestrian Mall in hopes of seeing a black Saints hat. He realizes the odds of that happening are slim to none, but figures that while he's getting a feel for the area, he might as well keep an eye out for his man.

He pauses for a moment and just takes it all in. The size of the area him and Hawk will have to cover with their eyes in order to find each other in a really huge crowd, is daunting!

He says to himself…"Man, this could be a real nightmare trying to find him in this mess! God help me!"

He moves on and continues looking around, always thinking; *"Come on Hawk! Be there! Just show up, man!!!"* He walks aimlessly, hoping against hope. It's not going to happen tonight.

CHAPTER 13

HAWK AT TIMES SQUARE

As the shadows are busy tailing their subjects, they send video to the Crew members every fifteen minutes in order for them to see what's going on. It keeps everyone well connected to the action on the street. So far, there's nothing exciting to see or report. Each team keeps track of their guy and makes sure no one messes with him. What they're guarding really, is a $200,000 fortune.

Crew man Malich is on the two-way radio and asks how Hawk is doing.

Shadow Joe reports. "We're still on the bus and are about ten minutes from the Square. I'll send video when we get there."

The bus finally stops a block from the Square. Hawk gets off and is followed by Joe. And, from the nice comfortable van he's been in while following the bus, new shadow, Chris, takes his place in surveilling Hawk's movements. Now that they're on foot, it'll be a little easier maintaining a safe distance between shadows and subjects.

They follow Hawk until he gets right into Times Square. It's the second week of April and crews are getting things ready for a concert scheduled for the following day when George and Hawk will need to make contact. That means there'll be a huge crowd in the Square and Pedestrian Mall. This will make things much more difficult for the two to find each other …maybe impossible!

Joe sees his subject looking around, probably trying to see if he can spot anyone with a Saints baseball cap. But like George, he too realizes that it's a long shot. Not being real familiar with the area, he stops a man and asks where the Pedestrian Mall is. He's shown where it is and starts heading there.

As he's walking, he looks at everyone who has on a black baseball cap, hoping to see a Saints cap. He sees a lot of guys near him wearing black caps but no one with the Saints logo. So far, he's only looked at the guys in his immediate area.

He says to himself, "This is incredible!" Then, a bit louder, *"Në:gë:h do'ogwenyö;h!"* (This is impossible!) He shakes his head and thinks, *Look at all these people! If I find George in this place, it'll be a miracle!*

There's no way for him to know if George is even there right now. He's aware that he'll only have tomorrow to find him and make it to the bank by 3 pm to complete the deal. That means they'll need to find each other before three o'clock – in a huge crowd. That worries him a lot! It seemed easy enough when it was first presented to him, but now that he's standing in the middle of the Square, it scares him! It's such a huge place with so many people.

CHAPTER 14

SHADOWS DOING THEIR JOB

It's now five o'clock. He's hungry and getting very tired. He has a few dollars in his pocket and goes to a nearby deli to buy a sandwich and a Coke. His shadow Chris is joined by another, Paul. They'll be his night shadows. They're hungry too and Chris follows Hawk into the deli to get something for himself and his partner. He stays a few steps behind Hawk, being careful not to be seen by him. He has no clue whatsoever that he's being tailed. That's good! The shadows are doing a great job. Hawk gets his food and exits the deli. He's being watched by Paul who has positioned himself a few doors down; staying well-hidden.

Chris leaves the deli with his own food and looks around to see that his partner has moved. He figures he's following their subject. He reaches him on his two-way device and is told where to catch up to him. Hawk has settled on a bench across the street and has begun eating his meal.

The shadows reunite in a darkened area about a hundred feet from their man and feast on their own take-out food. They see Hawk taking his time eating as he keeps looking at all the people near and far from him, just in case his man should come into view. Both shadows are also engaged in looking out for Georgie as they chomp down their sandwiches.

While George is still wandering the Pedestrian Mall, his shadows Everett and Hutch are doing their duty by informing the Crew what he's doing and where he is. So far, all is going well. The only thing that needs to be done right now is getting relief for them.

George's new shadows

The night shadows for George will be Tony and Max. They check in with the Crew and get ready to do what the others have done since 1 pm when Hawk and George were dropped off with their envelope containing the check and instruction sheet.

Jacques activates his two-way and says to the shadows who were on the first shift, "Hey guys, great job so far in tailing our two subjects. Go get some rest! You well deserve it. We'll see you in the morning. Have a great night. *Bonne nuit.*"

Fritz responds, "Thanks boss! See you in the morning." Joe, Everett, and Hutch click in and bid the Crew good night as well.

The new guys, Chris and Paul for Hawk, Tony and Max for George have the easy part now. They won't have to travel by subway or bus to stay with their subjects.

As the new shadows take over, they hear Sergio on their two-way, "Welcome aboard gentlemen! Stay sharp, and let us know if anything interesting comes up!"

Paul clicks back… "Thanks boss. We'll certainly report any new activity if there is any. Have a good night."

SALT AND PEPPER MYSTERY

George has already walked around Times Square and the Pedestrian Mall. He even checked out a place where he can be above the crowd to look down on them and have a better angle to spot that Saints cap Hawk will be wearing. He's now standing at 7th and 56th Street looking around to get a visual layout of the area. He crosses the street and heads toward a place called Charley's Eatery. It's supper time; he's hungry and has to get something to eat.

He enters the restaurant and a few minutes later, Tony and Max come in and sit at a table that is farthest from him. They keep their guy in view at all times and send a video of the inside of the place, showing where George is sitting.

It's nearing 7:30 pm when he finishes eating. Before getting up to put on his London Fog, Max observes him taking the larger than normal salt shaker, unscrewing the cap and pouring the entire content into the right hand pocket of his coat. He does the same thing with the pepper shaker … same pocket. Both men look at each other with a puzzled look, shrug their shoulders and chuckle quietly. He then gets up and goes to the register to pay his bill.

SHADOWS DOING THEIR JOB

Tony made his way out the door when he saw him getting ready to leave. He's hidden himself a couple of doors from the eatery waiting to see where George will go. Via his two-way radio, he lets Max know where to find him.

There's no way of knowing what George will do next. They simply follow and observe his every move. They hope he'll soon find a place to settle down and call it a night. It's a pretty boring time so far, except for the salt and pepper thing. That was somewhat amusing. They're still wondering what the heck he plans to do with it – all mixed together like that.

George feels he's scouted out the area well enough where he needs to be tomorrow to try and find Hawk. He's calling it a day. His concern right now is finding a place to sleep for the night. He's really tired and thinks about going to one of the nearby missions, but knows that they frisk everybody. They'd surely find the envelope under his shirt. He couldn't chance that.

He takes another short tour by Times Square as he makes his way to the Knickerbocker Hotel not far from there. During the time he worked as a carpenter, he'd been inside to do work and is familiar with the place. He plans on spending the night there in some out of the way corner in the basement. Tony and Max figure that's where their man will sleep. They hope that he'll stay put for the night.

George blends in well with the people in the lobby and heads for the staircase that leads to the basement where he knows there are large storage rooms. He's pretty sure no one will need to go there tonight. He slips inside one of them, finds an old sofa the hotel has stored there, and settles in. It's 9:00 pm. It's been a long day for him. In about a half hour, he's out like a light.

Tony and Max can only monitor him on their scanner now. They'll know if he moves. There will be a soft beeping from their scanner and a glowing blip showing movement. They call for one of their tricked out vans to come to their location so they can have nice reclining seats where they'll take turn standing watch while the other sleeps. In the morning, they'll resume the pursuit.

HAWK'S ACCOMMODATIONS

It's Hawk's turn to bed down. He's on the move looking for an abandoned building where he can stash himself. This won't be the first time he's had to find a place to sleep outside of a homeless shelter. He spots a vacant store and goes around the back to find a way in. Usually, places like that have been used by other homeless people before. He goes to the rear of the building, sees a boarded up window, pulls off the plywood and hops inside. He puts the plywood back up so that it doesn't look like it's been tampered with. He has a small flashlight and shines it around to be sure no one else is in there. After scouting out the store and finding a suitable spot where he can sleep, he settles in. It won't be very comfortable, but at least, he'll be safe and out of the cold, damp night.

As with George's shadows, Hawk's men, Chris and Paul radio in and tell the Crew that their man is "all tucked in." They call for a van to pick them up and park nearby. They are also equipped with the same tracking gear as George's crew. If Hawk moves during the night, they'll know.

After hearing the report on Hawk, Blanchard comes on the radio and says, "Okay everyone! We've had a long day. Great job! *Merci beaucoup*! Thank you! It pretty much went as I expected. Tomorrow will be a whole new ball game. For tonight, stay sharp! Anything can happen and we need to be ready for any unforeseen events. I'm going to sleep on the streets myself…in a nice roomy van. Good night."

The other two from the Crew, Rick and Sergio, each click on and add their own, "Thanks fellas! Good job and good night."

Most of the men in the Crew and all the others involved in this unprecedented adventure are not getting a good night's sleep. This is something none of them would have ever thought of being involved in. It's been an interesting day. Most of the men toss and turn as thoughts bounce around in their heads about the day and what might happen tomorrow. They all end up cat-napping at first, but one by one they eventually fall sound asleep.

Chapter 15

Geoge and Hawk - Up and at "em

It's 6 am of day three. Rick has already spoken to Jacques and Sergio by phone. Jacques asked him to contact all the men to make sure they're ready to take on the day. He does, and everyone responds affirmatively. They're ready to monitor their subjects.

Sergio comes through everyone's ear piece and says, "Top o' the mornin' to you, lads! Hope you all had a good night's sleep! Today should be a very interesting day. We're confident George and Hawk will find each other. The more interesting part will be what will happen after the initial meeting. The chip in their Saint Christopher medal has provided us with their exact location, and when we see them together, we'll activate their mics. Stay sharp, men."

At 7:10, the first of the two subjects to show a blip on the scanner is Hawk. At this time of year, the temperature in the building without heat is about 50 degrees. Good thing he's wearing a heavy coat. He makes his way out through the window, goes down the alleyway and onto the sidewalk. He figures George is either up or getting up and that he'll need to get to Pedestrian Mall and Times Square area as soon as he can.

He sees a corner food vender called the "Snack Box" and buys himself a large black cup of coffee and a couple of Danish pastries. He stops at a corner near the Pedestrian Mall where there's a newspaper dispenser and uses the top as a make-shift table for his coffee and the other Danish.

All the while he's having his breakfast his eyes scan the entire area in hopes of seeing a black Saints hat. No one comes into view. His daytime shadows, Joe and Fritz have positioned themselves close by, but not too close. It could happen that in scanning the crowd, Hawk could see one of them and if he should happen to see him again as he looks for George, it might very well send up a red flag. That could cause a problem. The shadows are pros at what they do and know how to be invisible. That's why the Crew picked them.

It's nearly 7:15 by the time George wakes up to voices in the hallway off the storage room where he spent the night. His spot was warmer than that of Hawk's. He gets up, goes to the door and listens to hear if anyone is out there. Confident the hall is clear, he opens the door a bit and sees a maid rummaging through her room cleaning cart a couple of doors down. Good thing for him, her back is turned and he's able to sneak away unnoticed.

He makes his way to the lobby and goes out the nearest exit. Once outside, with shadows Everett and Hutch in pursuit, he begins to walk toward Times Square. Just like Hawk, he needs a coffee to start his day. He spots a food vender, buys a coffee and breakfast sandwich similar to an Egg McMuffin. But, unlike Hawk, he doesn't stop to eat and drink. He has his breakfast on the move, searching the crowd for that "fleur-de-lis" on the Saints cap.

Both men realize they only have until 3 pm to connect. They're a bit stressed as they head toward the Square. At this time of the morning, 7:30, the area is already very busy. There's already a ton of people in the Square; people going to work, a stage crew setting up for the concert, shop and restaurant owners going in early to get ready to open, policemen patrolling on foot and horseback, lots of tourists, and many street people. It's crazy.

Chapter 16

Everybody on the Street

It's been nice for Jacques, Rick and Sergio to be riding in a comfortable van, but since George and Hawk are now in the same area, they want to be as the shadows are. Jacques and his friends are told exactly where the two subjects are right now. They want to do a "walk-by" of each man at a safe distance; just to get closer to the action and get a feel of what it's like being in that crowd.

Sergio makes his way towards Hawk, while Rick and Jacques head for where George is at the moment. After a couple of minutes Sergio sees that Hawk is finishing his second Danish. He moves in and positions himself only a few feet behind him. As Hawk moves, he moves, always maintaining a safe distance. As he watches his subject looking over the crowd, he notices the heavy frown on his face, like a man in deep anguish.

He radios to Jacques and Rich, "Hey fellas, poor Hawk is really stressed out! I wish I could help him. We'll just wait and see what happens. I hope for his sake that he finds George soon."

Rick clicks back and says, "Hopefully, it'll be well before three o'clock."

GUTSY ENCOUNTER

Jacques and Rick have made their way close to their target. They see George sipping his coffee, and like Hawk, he's scanning the crowd for that same cap. It's like trying to find a needle in haystack. It's early, but there are a lot of people out there already, a couple thousand, maybe. The city is expecting between five and seven thousand people by mid-day. The concert is scheduled for 3 pm.

Rich says to Jacques, "Watch this!" He walks over to George, taps him on the shoulder and asks, "Excuse me sir, but do you have the time?"

George doesn't even look at him. He keeps scanning the crowd; he can't afford to be distracted right now. He realizes that if he loses his spot in scanning the people; he could miss Hawk.

Without looking at Rick, he says to him in a very abrupt tone, "I don't know! I don't have a watch! Go ask somebody else!"

Rick could hear the stress in his voice by the way he spoke to him, and says, "Thanks anyway, pal. Have a great day!"

George says nothing. Still not looking at him, he only puts his hand up as if to say, "Yeah, thanks!"

With that, Rick steps back, rejoins Jacques and says to him, "What did you think of that, old buddy?"

Jacques smiles at him in an approving way and says, "Pretty ballsy! I'm impressed! I'll have to try that myself. I can't have you outdo me!"

They both laugh and continue their surveillance. The upside of this little dare is that George didn't get a look at Rick. His identity is still safe.

After a few minutes of tailing him, they can see that he's become very aggravated because he can't seem to get a good view of the crowd. They see him look to his left at a raised spectator stand in the Square and watch him make his way there. They follow at a fair distance, but not too far. They don't want to lose track of him in the crowd. It could easily happen.

George makes his way up the stand. It brings him to a perfect perch that overlooks the entire area where Hawk could be walking. He couldn't have found a better spot to look for him.

Jacques, on his two-way radio says, "Hey men, Georgie has a great place to look for Hawk. He's standing against the railing at the top of the spectator stand. Check him out! He's wearing a London Fog coat. Anybody see where Hawk is right now?"

Fritz says, "Yeah boss, he's out there in the crowd about seven hundred feet or so in front of the stand; a bit to the left. Where are you sir?"

"Seven hundred feet, you say. That's quite a distance for them to make eye contact, even to get a clear look at the 'Fleur-de-lis' on the cap. Rick and I are standing near the food vendor in the shadow of the stand and can see George clearly. I'm sure he won't look down here as he scans the crowd trying to find Hawk. Do you see us?"

"Roger that sir. I see you."

At around 11:35, as George is busy scanning the crowd, two young grungy punks approach him and one guy tells him to hand over his money.

George thinks, *WHAT, again! That's twice in two days.*

He tells them, "I don't have any money, man! Leave me alone!"

The shadows are close by and see that there's a confrontation. Everett, who is a good size man, makes his way towards them and as one of the perps puts his hand on George, he grabs it and twists it to the point of nearly snapping his wrist.

He tells them, "Beat it before I break both your necks!"

The two would-be thieves are smaller and see that they're no match for him. They quickly back off, head down the viewing stand, and mix in with the crowd.

Hutch, keeps his eyes on them in case they look like they're going to hang around and come back when George's helper leaves.

He isn't too shaken and thanks Everett for stepping in. He says to him, "Thanks for the help, man! I could've handled one guy, but two of them would've been a problem."

Ev tells George to take care, and as he's leaving, he looks around to make sure the two punks are nowhere nearby. He doesn't see them. He radios Hutch, "More than likely, they'll target another lone unfortunate soul in the crowd."

While walking away from the scene, he hears Hutch in his ear piece say, "I've got my eyes on those two idiots, Ev. They're headed away from the stand. George should be okay now." He adds, "Apparently, that London Fog coat is attracting misfits! That's twice he's been messed with. He must look like he's got money."

As Everett heads to a place where he can be hidden from George's view again, he says, "You're right Hutch, that's two times too many. And… right again about that coat; maybe Georgie should lose it."

The Crew saw what went on. Rick's voice comes on the two-way. "Great cover Ev! So glad you were there to handle that problem. It means a lot to this operation. Keep up the good work."

He responds, "Thanks boss! It was good stepping in and doing more than just standing around watching our man's movements. We'll keep you posted, sir."

It is 11:45. George is very aggravated that the robbery attempt has disrupted his scanning of the crowd and thinks, *Man! I hope I didn't miss seeing Hawk while that was going on! If I did, this could really set me back! Damn it! DAMN IT!!! This is impossible! God help me! PLEASE! Hawk where ARE you?*

Now, he's really upset that he lost his spot in the search. He whispers to himself, "Come on Saints hat! Where the hell are you?!" He keeps looking.

Hawk, being taller than most people, just keeps eyeing the heads of guys around him, looking for a black cap, any black cap. Finally, he sees one that could be what he's looking for. The guy has his back to him. He walks quickly through the crowd, bumping people and excusing himself, but always keeping his eyes on the target. He reaches the man, taps him on the shoulder and says, "Excuse me! Is your name George?"

The man turns and says, "No! My name's Wally, Wally Black."

As he says that, Hawk can see that the front of the cap doesn't have the Saints emblem. With a very disappointing look on his face, he says, "Never mind... sorry I bothered you, man!"

Desperation pushed him to do what he just did. He wants so bad for this hunt to be over; to find George and for the two of them to be on their way to the bank to get their money. He knows it was a bad move. He realizes he's lost time, and now, he's extremely angry with himself for having done that ...but gets right back to scanning the crowd. It's an impossible task. There's no technique to his search. He's just looking left, right, left, right, left, right.

His thoughts are, *If George is moving around like I am, among all these people, we may not find each other by three o'clock, or maybe not till tonight. Then, it'll be too late, and there goes my $100,000! God, help me!*

Now, he's getting really desperate because there isn't much time left for him and George to make it to the bank! His breathing becomes labored and his heart is beating faster. He has that look of an extremely agitated man at this point. The search has almost pushed him to the point of giving up. His emotions are all over the place. He says, "Në:gë:h de ' tge:i '!" (This isn't right!") It can't be that I did all this and won't be able to find George in time to get that $100,000."

Although he's completely demoralized, he's not one to give up and keeps looking for that Saints cap.

Luckily, George is on his perch well above the crowd and has the best view of the people below. He doesn't even think of leaving that spot and going down into that mess of people. He knows that if he did, it would be a truly impossible search. So... he stays, and keeps looking.

The Crew is also aware that George has chosen the right place to look for Hawk. They figure that the men are close enough to each other now that one of them should spot that "fleur-de-lis" soon! It's only a matter of time...but, time that is quickly ticking away.

FINALLY! CONTACT

It's nearly 1:05; about an hour and a half has passed since George was accosted by the two punks and he's getting extremely anxious. He's almost ready to move to another part of the platform when, all of a sudden...he sees the hat! They're about five hundred feet from each other.

He has to squint to get a better look and says to himself, "That's GOTTA be my man! There's that black baseball cap with the Saints logo! Thank you, Lord!"

From his vantage point, he keeps his eyes on where Hawk is, but realizes that if he leaves his spot and goes down into the crowd to connect with him, not knowing which way Hawk might turn and walk, he could lose him. He decides to stay put and signal him from where he is... figuring that anyone looking out toward the platform would be able to see him waving. He waits for Hawk to look his way. He's even more anxious than before. He hopes Hawk will not turn and start walking away from him. He waits and prays.

Hawk is standing in one spot in the sea of people. He keeps looking around, searching for any sign of his guy. Ironically, at one point, his gaze passes right by George. He doesn't see him! Seeing that, George goes crazy and is waving like a lunatic to make Hawk see him. He's looking left now, and... as his head slowly turns back to look straight ahead, he looks up and sees a guy waiving frantically at the top of the stand! George sees that he's spotted him, and both men get a huge grin on their face as if to say... "FINALLY! George motions for him to come toward the side of the stand; that would put him directly below him. Hawk moves as quickly as he can to get through the thick crowd.

Jacques notes the time, it is 1:20. He says, *"Mais ça c'est bon!"* (Man, this is good!).

He and the others in the Crew are talking it up on their two-way after seeing what just happened. Everyone is thrilled. The hunt is over!

He radios to all the guys, "This is great, gentlemen! I'm so glad they finally found each other! Although it's the end of this part of the pursuit, it'll be interesting to see what happens next with the face to face meeting. Our subjects are about to meet. Stay sharp men! We don't know what's going to happen, but we'll know real soon."

Chapter 17

The face to face

After fighting his way through several hundred people with his hand tight over his breast pocket, in case of pick pockets, he finally gets close enough to speak to George. He says to him, "Are you George?"

"Yes! I am… and, you gotta be Hawk, right?"

"Yes! I'll come up to where you are."

Georgie tells him, "No, no, don't move! Stay right where you are! I'm coming down."

He makes his way down the stairs, comes to where Hawk is waiting and asks him if he's wearing a medal. He pulls out his Saint Christopher; just enough to show it to him, then drops it back inside his shirt. George does the same. This assures both men that they are dealing with the right person. They shake hands and George gives Hawk a huge hug.

The Crew and shadows see what's going on and wait to see what the subjects do next. The microphones in the medals are activated and everyone listens in.

They hear George say, "Man, I'm so glad we finally connected. I was getting real worried we wouldn't find each other in time."

Hawk leans down to talk in George's ear and says, "Me too! But now that we hooked up, let's get going! We don't have a whole lot of time left, only an hour and a half. Let's get away from the crowd so we can hear each other better. We need to talk, man."

They head towards Bryant Park, which is a little more than a block from Times Square and go to a quiet spot.

George tells Hawk, "Let me see your half of the check!"

As he pulls the envelope from his coat, he pauses and asks George to do the same with his.

George hesitates and says, "I don't have it with me, it's somewhere safe."

In a very angry tone, Hawk says to him, "What the HELL do you mean you don't have the check on you?! You BETTER not have lost it, man! I'll break your neck if you did!!! We're talkin' about $200,000 here, man!"

With Hawk being so angry, George doesn't know if he's going to get punched out. He backs away and motions for him to calm down.

He tells him without being specific, "I hid it yesterday near the bank. I didn't want to take a chance on being robbed of such a valuable thing when I slept or as I made my way to find you.

Trust me! It's in a real safe place. You'll really be amazed when you see where I hid it. Now then, let's get a look at that check. Come on man, I gotta see it!"

Hawk is still really angry about the whole thing but takes the half check out of the envelope and shows it to him.

George looks at it, smiles broadly and says, "Man, we're gonna be rich in a little while!"

Although he doesn't have his part of the check, he quickly pulls his envelope from the inside of his shirt and shows Hawk the yellow instruction sheet. This verifies that he is who he says he is.

That being done, they start walking toward a bus stop to get to the bank. George tells Hawk all about the episode of having lost the instruction sheet and how he got it back.

Hawk stops, looks at him and says, "Man…! You're real lucky you found that sheet! If you hadn't, you and I wouldn't be talking right now and we'd both be out $100,000! It makes me sick to even think about it!"

George says to him, "Makes YOU sick! Man, you can't imagine what I went through after realizing I didn't have that sheet. I just about went nuts!!! I died inside, man!"

"Well, we're good now," says Hawk, "and in a little more than an hour and half, we'll get our dough. We're losing valuable time standing here. Let's get to that bank, partner!"

Chapter 18

Getting to the bank

Everett and Hutch tail George and Hawk as they walk down 41st Street to catch a bus on 9th Avenue that will take them south to City Businessmen's Bank on 9th and 20th; a twenty block ride. The shadows are going to have to be very slick staying with their subjects without raising any "red flags." While waiting for their ride, they've positioned themselves jut right to make boarding happen without a hitch.

The bus pulls up and everyone gets on. George and Hawk pick a seat toward the back that faces sideways. This way, they can see people coming and going with no one sitting behind them. They're being very cautious, not trusting anyone. At this point, being so close to their goal, they leave nothing to chance. Both men keep a sharp eye for anyone who might even look suspicious.

The two shadows have taken seats close enough to intervene in case of trouble. Everett is sitting diagonally across from them pretending he's reading messages on his cell phone. Hutch is at the very back of the bus so he can see the entire crowd from front to back. Their subjects are well covered.

TROUBLE ON THE BUS

New York can be a really good city, but there are always people who are bent on disturbing the peace. As it turns out, after only traveling seven blocks, three brain-dead older teens spot our two peaceful bus riders and object that they're wearing New Orleans Saints caps. One is a tall black kid, then there's a shorter portly white boy with a hard-guy look in his face, and the other, an average height Hispanic, looking tough. All are wearing New York Giants caps.

The Hispanic kid speaks up and says, "Hey you two maricones... you tryin' to disrespect us by wearin' those Saints hats in OUR city? You better lose them or we'll cut you, man!"

Hawk says, *"O:ya' ketgë haksá'a:h!"* ("Another bad boy!") He gets ready for action.

George has his right hand in his coat pocket, the one containing a mixture of salt and pepper. He grabs a handful and readies himself. As the punks go inside their coats for their knives, quick as lightning, in a sweeping motion, he throws his concoction in the faces of all three misguided lads and gets them right in the eyes! They scream in pain and can't see their victims. Hawk happens to be wearing steel-tipped construction boots. He gets up and kicks the two closest to him in the shins with sufficient force to crack their tibias and pushes the third guy, making him stagger backward into Hutch's lap. The driver sees the commotion in his rear view mirror and stops.

Hutch yells to him, "Driver, open the door back here!"

He opens it. George, Hawk and Hutch toss the punks out onto the sidewalk where they continue writhing in extreme pain. George's weapon worked like a charm; the boys' eyes are on fire. The driver closes the door and pulls away. The way it all happened allowed Hutch to keep his cover. George and Hawk haven't a clue that he's there to watch their backs.

George says to him, "Thanks for the help, man. Much appreciated."

He replies, "It was nothing. Glad I could help. Punks like that need a good ass-kicking now and then. By the way, what the heck was it you threw at them?"

"Oh, nothing much, just plain old salt and pepper mixed together. I always keep some in my right coat pocket. This way, I have my own brand of pepper spray. In my case, it becomes a 'salt and pepper toss.' As you just saw, it works great mixed together like that."

Without letting on that he knows where George got the salt and pepper toss, Hutch says, "That's very clever! I'll have to keep that in mind. More people in this city should learn to do that. It's a great self-defense tactic."

He shakes Hawk's and George's hand, tells them to take care and heads back to his seat. Since he's had this little bit of interaction with them, he'll need to have another shadow take his place to avoid being seen at later stake-outs. Everett sent the entire episode from his cell phone for the Crew to see. He was able to hear cheering in his earpiece as it all went down.

Rick comes on the two-way and says, "Like Jacques said… anything can happen. This was one of those cases. Glad you guys are there. Things could have gone really bad had our subjects been knifed." Then, he comments on the salt and pepper thing. "So… that's why he poured all the salt and pepper in his pocket at the restaurant! I like that. That's pretty ingenious. Okay guys, all is well. Keep up the good work."

As the men continue their trek toward the bank, Hawk turns to George and says in a hushed voice, "Hey partner, how about we don't wear these hats? We only needed them so we could I.D. each other in the crowd. The instructions didn't say anything about us needing to wear them after we found each other. We don't need them anymore. What do you say?"

George leans in and says, "You're right big guy, we don't need them anymore and we certainly don't need anyone else screwing with us on our trip to the bank. Wearing Saints hats in this town isn't a good idea. Let's lose them!"

Both men take off their cap, roll it up and tuck it inside their coat. They sit back and keep an eye out for their stop.

ANOTHER BUMP IN THE ROAD

This little bus ride is not a good one. About ten blocks away from the bank, some drunk gets on and sits right across from our soon-to-be rich guys. This goofball just keeps staring at Hawk and doesn't let up!

After a few minutes of staring at him with a menacing look, he blurts out, "Hey Cochise… shouldn't you be on a horse instead of riding this bus?"

Hawk shakes his head and says to himself, *"Age:h!… neh o:yá hainy ö 'öh!"* ("Oh no, another [bad] white guy!")

He grins and says, "Cochise! He was a great man. He's one of my heroes. Thanks for the compliment. And, as for my horse, he's being shoed at the moment so I thought I'd ride this big iron horse today. Is that okay with you?"

"What I'd really like you to do is…get off my bus!" says the drunk.

George jumps in and says to Hawk, "What do you think… a little salt and pepper for this hombre?"

Hawk tells him, "Nah! Our stop is coming up real soon. We're going to let him sleep it off."

George looks at him a bit puzzled. Hawk winks at him. He figures his buddy has something in mind. Their stop is just ahead. They both get up and get ready to get off. As they're standing in front of the idiot who is still wearing his bad guy game-face and mumbling more ethnic insults, Hawk hits him with a stiff elbow to the jaw and knocks him out.

George turns to him and says, "I guess that's what you meant by 'letting him sleep it off', eh? Good one, Cochise!"

"Yep, he's just some doofus needing a little lesson and time to sleep off the booze. Man, I can't wait to get the hell out of this city! Let's get to the bank! Where is it, pale face?"

George tells him that they're only about two blocks away. Both men are really anxious to get there. Finally, they've arrived.

The bus stops, the two get off and begin walking toward the bank. Everett gets off too. He's not had any close range personal interaction with George and Hawk. He didn't get in the mix with the three punks when Hutch did. Hutch stays aboard and radios for a new man to take his place. Having anticipated a need for replacements, the Crew has Fritz join Everett in following the men to the bank.

With security cameras covering just about every inch of the bank, the shadows will need to be extra discreet in sending video feeds from there. They're pros and will know how to do it without being detected.

CHAPTER 19

INSIDE THE BANK

The men have now made their way to the doors of the City Businessmen's Bank. As they enter, George looks back toward the street and notices a police squad car with north precinct markings on it and a plain-clothes man sitting behind the wheel.

He finds it odd and thinks, *That cruiser is way out of its district. I wonder what it's doing here in Lower Manhattan?*

For now, he lets it go and walks in with his partner. It's a very large bank with a lot of customers doing business. That's good. It'll help with what he needs to do next. He leads Hawk toward the counter where he hid his half of the check, but there's a slight problem. There are several people using the counter, with one man standing right where he needs to go. They'll have to wait till he leaves.

This makes Hawk feel really out of place. He's very uncomfortable being in the presence of mostly business people. He felt uneasy just walking in the place. It's not a "regular people's bank," it's for business people and high finance folks. He stands out like a sore thumb; big Indian guy with a pony tail, wearing blue-jeans, construction boots and a Navy Pea-coat.

They stand near the counter and wait for the man to get done. Both are anxious and worry they'll draw attention to themselves if they're seen just standing around and not conducting any business. The two do have business to conduct, and it will happen as soon as they can get to the corner of that counter. George gets his partner to pretend they're carrying on a conversation… just in case the security guys have their eyes on them.

Luck is on their side. The customer finishes in only a couple of minutes. George moves in quickly and Hawk follows. He has his tall friend shield him at the corner of the counter where he hid his half of the check. The guys in the security room watching the cameras won't see what he's doing. He's quick about it. He reaches to the back, pulls up a small bank envelope and lays it down on the counter. Hawk puts his hand to his mouth to hide the huge smile he has. He remembers when George told him, *"You'll really be amazed where I hid it."*

He whispers to him, "I can't believe you put your half right here in the bank…taped to the back of a counter! You're either a genius or completely crazy, man!"

George responds, "I AM a genius… AND, crazy… like a fox! It worked didn't it, Cochise?"

"Yes it did my pale-face friend. Now, let's finish this thing! I can't wait to get my money and get out of here! This place makes me feel real uneasy, man."

This is a real special moment! He tells Hawk to take out his check. He does. George takes his half out of the envelope and puts it on the counter next to Hawk's half so they can get a look at what the entire check says.

There it is! *"Pay to the bearers two hundred thousand dollars and 00/100 cents."*

Both men smile at each other. Hawk gives him a one arm hug and says, "Let's go see our Mister Druitt and get our dough, shall we?"

George nudges his partner and points to where the office is. They walk to the receptionist's desk and George asks the secretary to tell Mr. Druitt that the two men he's waiting for are here for their three o'clock appointment. She calls on the interoffice phone and gives him the message.

After about thirty seconds, she hangs up and tells the men, "Mr. Druitt will be with you in a moment. He needs to place a couple of important phone calls first." With a smile, she motions them to a sitting area and says, "Please have a seat and wait till he comes for you, it shouldn't be long."

It's now 3:05. While they wait, out of the corner of his eye, George notices some guy looking at him and Hawk. He pretends he doesn't see him as he scans the people in the bank. As soon as the guy turns away to make a call, George tells Hawk to stay put, that he has to check out something. He gets up and makes his way nonchalantly behind the pillar where the man is standing. He's close enough to hear his cell phone conversation.

"Yeah captain, I'm in the bank and have my eyes on the two guys. I'll wait for Druitt to signal you, and in turn, you can let me know if they'll be leaving with the money. Then, we'll take the next step to relieve them of their loot."

George gets back quickly to Hawk and says, "Hey, nice and easy like, at your left, take a quick glance at the guy way over there by that pillar. He's been eyeing us. He was talking to some captain on his phone. I figure him to be some bad guy put in play to do us in. I heard him mention 'two guys' and 'relieving them of the loot.' We're two guys… and… we're about to get a lot of money."

Hawk gets a quick look at him and turns back to hear George continue….

"He also mentioned Druitt on the phone. Druitt had to make an important phone call just before seeing us. I'm figuring he was calling that captain, whoever he is, and I'm guessing they're waiting till we have our money, then make their move once we hit the street. This is not good, buddy. I feel we may have been setup!"

Hawks says, "So…you think Druitt and some cop have something shady going on? We're going to have to think of something fast, Georgie! What do we do?"

George puts his index finger up, signaling Hawk to hold for a moment. He looks through Druitt's office window and sees him talking on the phone. He looks quickly at the man by the pillar and sees him listening to someone on his cell phone; now he's talking and Druitt is listening. To George, it's simple math.

He says to Hawk, "Yep, I believe there's something wrong here my friend. I think there's a three-way conversation going on. Remember the caution we got in the instructions about 'trusting no one!' Well, here it is. We can't trust anyone here! We need to outsmart these weasels. Let's see how Druitt deals with us. He may regard us as 'mere bums,' but us knowing that he's involved somehow gives us the upper hand. Let's wait and see what happens when we meet with him."

They see Druitt hang up, and both men look at the guy tailing them just as he shuts off his cell phone. They look at each other and nod as if to say, "Aha! Got you!"

Being that everyone can hear everything that Hawk and George say via the mics in their Saint Christopher medal, Everett who is inside the bank speaks in his sleeve mic and says, "Boss, I'm sure you heard what our subjects have just discovered. What do you think?"

Jacques replies, "Let's wait and see what Druitt tells our guys. We won't let them get ripped off. I want to see what George and Hawk end up doing to foil Druitt and our unknown accomplice's evil scheme! Keep your eyes on the perp in the bank while our soon-to-be rich men have their meeting with Druitt. I'm having a hard time believing our banker would be involved in any kind of a scam. I surely hope he isn't. He's not the type of man that would be part of ripping me off. We've known each other too long. On the other hand, there are a couple of captains in the city who are crooked. Right now, I suspect one in particular, Captain Bates from the north precinct. He sort of knows about the adventure we're on. I heard he's put the squeeze on a few citizens before for his own personal gain. I wouldn't be surprised if he's got something on Druitt. I'll get a friend of mine run a police check on him to see if anything comes up. He may have a DWI or some other embarrassing thing in his past that Bates is using to force him into something shady. Let's see if I'm right."

Chapter 20

George, Hawk and Druitt

As the Crew keeps close tabs on George and Hawk, Druitt finally invites them into his office. It's now 3:25 pm. He asks that they show him the check. Each man lays his half on the desk. Druitt takes a look at them to verify they're a match. He turns over the two pieces, tapes them together and directs the men to sign their names. Eagerly, Hawk takes the pen and signs his, then George.

Druitt says their names, "John Hawkeye, George Freeman. Very good! Now, we'll proceed and finalize the transaction gentlemen." He reaches in a box on the floor next to his desk, brings up two very nice canvas bags and says, "Here are special canvas shoulder bags for you to carry your money in when we're done."

George says to him, "Oh no, I won't be taking ALL my money with me today. I'll only take a couple of hundred and leave the rest in an account here at your bank." With a smile, he adds,

"And, I'd like to have that fine canvas bag if that's okay! It's very cool-looking; it'll go really nice with my coat."

Hawk looks at him and rolls his eyes in a mocking way as if to say…"Really?"

Druitt has a look on his face that tells George he expected him to take all his money with him today. He figures that whoever is going to do the heist is expecting to hit both men and get the entire $200,000 in one fell swoop.

With George's decision to bank his money, the score would now only be half of the expected amount. Good for George, but a bummer for the thieves. Besides, he doesn't want to walk around anywhere in the city with that kind of cash in a shoulder bag. He realizes that as soon as they leave the bank, there very well could be someone waiting for the right chance to grab their fortune, especially after hearing the conversation of the guy on the cell phone. It's the wisest thing to do.

Clearing his throat, Druitt says, "Ahem…! Very well Mr. Freeman, I'll get my assistant to set up that account for you right away…and, here's your canvas bag."

He writes down what George wants done with the money on an interoffice form and calls the assistant manager with a request to come and assist a new customer in setting up an account. The assistant comes in and asks George to follow him to his office.

Before leaving, he tells Hawk, "Make sure I see you before you leave, okay?"

Hawk turns to him, winks and says, "Absolutely! I wouldn't think of leaving before we had a chance to talk."

He's left alone with Druitt to deal with his money and is asked what he'd like to do with it?

"I'm leaving the city tonight. I'll need to take all my money with me now. Is there any problem with that?"

"No, no problem Mr. Hawkeye. How would you like the cash divided; tens, twenties, hundreds? You tell me."

He pauses to think for a moment and says, "I want $99,500 in one hundred dollar bills; nine packs of $10,000 each, and one pack of $9,500. The $500 that's left over, I'll need that for pocket money in smaller denominations for my trip back home."

It's now 3:45 pm. Druitt tells him that it'll take about forty-five minutes or so to put everything together and that he must fill out specific forms for the withdrawal. He offers Hawk coffee, which he takes, then heads over to the accounting department next to his.

Fritz and Everett are watching everything from two locations in the bank and continue to radio the activities of all players involved. Fritz positions himself close to the accounting office and observes Druitt attaching some sort of "button" to Hawk's canvas bag. He radios the Crew with that bit of information.

Sergio says, "Georgie was right. Druitt is dirty! He planted something in the bag, most likely a tracking device. Keep a sharp eye out there, boys! This could get a bit complicated."

Jacques can't help but step in and says' "I'm very upset to see that my friend Druitt is actually involved in such a scheme. There's something very wrong here. I'll deal with him personally later."

And he says to everyone, "Gentlemen, we wanted an adventure, well we got one. Remember what I told you earlier about Hawk and George getting their money from the bank, *'that it may not be the end of our involvement.'* This just might be the most important part of this tale. I believe we're about to find out just how involved we'll need to be here. Stay alert guys!"

"Staying alert boss," says Everett. "I've got the bad guy in view. He's standing to the left of the front entrance and has his eyes on our subjects. I'll cover the front door. Fritz, go cover that side door in case Hawk and George go out that way and our bad guy has an accomplice out there."

George's business went smoothly…he's done. He has $200 in cash in his pocket and signed all the proper forms to set up an account for $99,800. It's nearly 4:20 pm. He's now in a customer waiting area and taking in all of the activity around him. He looks through the large glass doors at the front of the bank and notices the cop car is still parked there. This makes him nervous. He scans the bank for the captain's man and spots him near the front entrance. He looks over at the office where Hawk is still sitting while Druitt oversees the count of his money in the accounting department.

He sees one of the clerks in that office putting packets of cash through a counting machine. He figures it must be Hawk's cash. It shouldn't be much longer...

Sure enough, five minutes later, Druitt walks out of the accounting office with paperwork in hand and a canvas shoulder bag that looks like it has some weight to it. He goes in his office, shuts the door and closes the blinds. This final step needs privacy.

He takes out the cash from the bag so Hawk can check the count for himself. Each cash packet has a paper band around it with the amount. He also has a small bank envelope containing the $500 in smaller denomination that Hawk requested. He hands everything over and tells him to count it to make sure it's accurate. Hawk verifies that both the contents of the shoulder bag and the $500 have the correct amount.

He signs the bank forms put in front of him and Druitt says, "Mr. Hawkeye, this concludes our transaction. Good luck to you, sir!"

Hawk thanks him, puts the loose cash in his right front pocket, slings the bank bag over his left shoulder and walks out of the office.

As soon as he leaves, Druitt puts in a call to Mr. Blanchard to tell him the two men showed up and have their money. He tells him that only Hawk has taken all his cash with him and that George banked most of it. Jacques thanks him for helping with the process and that he'll be by next week to take him to lunch.

Chapter 21

Plan "B"

It's now 4:45 and the bank will be closing in fifteen minutes. George sees Hawk and waves him over. They come together at a counter in the corner of the bank that is to the left of Druitt's office.

He asks Hawk, "Did everything go okay? Did you get all your money?"

"Yeah, I got it all. Now I need to get myself to the bus station. I want to get home where I belong. Where's the nearest station Georgie?"

"The Port Authority bus station is about 18 blocks north of here on Eight Avenue and 42nd."

"Eighteen blocks huh? Man, that's a long way from here. Hey, where's the guy that was tailing us? Is he still around?"

"Yeah. He's over there at your six near the front door. When you left Druitt's office, I saw him make a couple of phone calls and as I looked at the cop's man, wouldn't you know it, he answered HIS cell. As Druitt hung up, that guy closed his cell and put it in his pocket."

He then says to him, "Cochise, I feel you're not clear to walk out of here and get on with your life to enjoy that money just yet."

Hawk looks at him and says angrily, "Man, I got my money and ready to light out of here to get my life back, and now I may have to deal with some thief! This STINKS!"

George grabs his arm and pulls him over to a spot away from people and tells him, "Hawk, I know it stinks! We just have to figure what to do next…and REAL quick! I'm okay to walk out of here, most of my money is safe, but you, you're definitely a target for bad guys. We can't let that happen. We won't let it happen! I'm with you till you get clear of danger, brother. I promise you!"

Hawk thanks him for doing that. He's never-the-less very irritated and says, "It's pretty sick, man! I'm trapped in a bank with $100,000 on me. I can't stay here, and when I leave I may lose it all to a corrupt cop. You got anything in mind?"

"I do. We still have a bit of time before the bank closes at 5 o'clock. They don't lock the doors until 5:30 in order to allow customers to finish their business. I always loved having a 'Plan B,' and I have one for this situation."

You're going to find this strange, but I feel my boy is looking out for his old man and is guiding me. While you were in Druitt's office and I went to the assistant's office to settle my account, I saw a photo of him and his son on a fishing trip. That triggered memories of me and Beau doing things together. As if guided by my boy, my gaze went to the right of the photo and I saw stacks of flyers pretty much the size of the money packets in your bag. This gave me an idea! I thought about this bad situation with the banker and cop and came up with the perfect solution."

He faces Hawk, opens his coat a little and whispers, "Check out what I have tucked in my shirt. I have some in my pockets too. I snatched them up when Druitt's assistant went to one of the tellers to get my cash."

Hawk sees the packs of bank pamphlets and says to him, "What the hell are you going to do with those? How are they supposed to help me?! What kind of 'Plan B' is this? I don't get it, man!"

He tells Hawk, "You gotta trust me, Cochise! What I have in mind will work. We'll go to the john so you can be out of everybody's view; you'll then switch the money in the bag for these. You can tuck all of your money in your shirt, pants, boots, and inside coat pockets. Let's go! It's going to be fine, I promise you."

They get to the restroom and fortunately, no one else is in there. They have the privacy they need to make the switch. Hawk quickly takes the money out of the bank sack and tucks it everywhere he can on his person while George puts the pamphlets in the sack. The captain's man knows that the only way out of there is the same door they went in. He's confident he won't lose them.

The switch is done within four minutes. They both come out and make their way to the main exit. Hawk holds on tight to the bag giving the impression to anyone watching him that he's guarding it well.

Having heard George and Hawk's conversation with regards to Plan "B," there's a quiet cheer going on in the minds of the Crew.

Jacques comes on the two-way, "WOW! That George is a really smart man. First, he foils two robbers with his decoy wallet, then used salt and pepper to blind the punks on the bus, and now he's pulled a misdirection act by switching Hawk's money for pamphlets. I like this guy! I like him a lot! I might just hire him after all this is over."

CHAPTER 22

LEAVING THE BANK

It's getting close to 5:30 and time to go. As George and Hawk go out the Ninth Avenue exit, the guard who is letting people out says to them very courteously, "Gentlemen, have a great evening."

This certainly isn't their best day. Besides worrying about being confronted by a thief or thieves, it's raining really hard outside. The best way to cover eighteen blocks to the bus station will be for them to catch a cab. They see one idling by the curb and head for it. George taps on the window, the driver waves them in. They climb aboard and tell the driver to take them to the bus terminal on 42nd and Eight Avenue. They feel safe now. So far so good, no sign of anything looking like trouble.

The driver says, "Since it is rush hour, I suggest we take 12th Avenue by the Hudson River where the traffic moves much faster and there won't be so many traffic lights."

George knows Hawk wants to get to the terminal as fast as he can so he can get home. He says, "The easiest and quickest route is what we want. That'll be great! Let's go!"

The cab heads towards West Street while the men sit back and do their best to relax.

Jacques, Rick and Sergio are following them in their chauffeur-driven high tech van with shadows behind them in two other similar vans. They're only a couple of cars behind the cab and are doing all they can to not lose them. They realize that if something can go sideways, this would be the time and place. In this rush hour traffic, a number of things could go wrong. This is the first time since the start of the adventure that the Crew and shadows have the possibility of losing their subjects.

Sergio says, "Too bad one of our armed men couldn't be in the cab with them. It sure would make me feel a lot more at ease."

"Yeah…that would be good," says Rick. "But then, it would take away from the suspense of how they'll actually do on their own. Let's hope nothing goes wrong. We'll just keep a good thought."

While moving along on 12th Avenue near the Hudson River, cars are constantly maneuvering to get ahead by changing lanes. This makes tailing this cab a real challenge.

As they continue their pursuit, some imbecile swerves in front of the lead van and causes a three car collision. All the vans are now stopped. Jacques' vehicle is bumper to bumper with the car that caused the accident and can't move. The others are able to back up enough to allow the Crew's van to maneuver and go around.

Jacques says to his driver, "Catch up to that cab! We can't lose it! We've lost valuable time and I'm NOT happy!"

His driver hits the gas and does his best to catch up but the traffic isn't moving very fast.

Serge says, "Thank God we have them on our monitor. Can you imagine if we didn't …and they ran into trouble?"

"This is NOT good!" says Jacques. "We've gotta catch up to them!"

On their screen, they can see that the cab is now over a half mile ahead. This interruption allowed more cars to get in front of them, creating an even bigger obstacle.

As the cabby continues at a good pace, someone rear-ends him just before they get to West 29th Street. He's forced to pull over. Hawk and George turn to get a look at the man through the back window as he gets out of his car. The rain makes it difficult to clearly see the blurry figure coming. They can only make out that he's a big guy wearing a long coat and hat. When he gets to the cab, the driver rolls down the window and is asked to turn into the construction site just ahead on the right so they can exchange insurance information. The man gets back in his car and follows the cab.

To Hawk and George, this seems a bit suspicious. They hope this is just a freak accident; that the two drivers will simply exchange information and be on their way. At this stage of the game, they don't need any more drama. Hawk just wants to go home and George would love nothing better than to head over to the mission to rest for the night. But as fate would have it, they're caught up in another situation, one that is completely out of their control. They don't know what to expect.

Both cars pull in the construction area and come to a stop around a large dump truck. The guy gets out of his car, walks to the cab, opens the rear door and points a .25 caliber pistol at them. It is equipped with a silencer. They're told to get out; Hawk goes first, then George.

This was a very well planned "bump and rob" tactic. He was able to trace them by the tracking device Druitt attached to the bag. The thief has them right where he wants them. Since the pistol-packing perp got word that only Hawk took his money from the bank in a canvas bag, he knows who to target. He could see that George's bag is empty by the lack of a bulge that would be seen if he had anything in it.

He says to Hawk, "You! Hand over that bag!"

He'd like to hit this jerk, but knows he can't beat a bullet. He does as he's told and hands it over. The guy snatches it and tells them to back up against the truck. He gets in his car, fires a couple of rounds at them through the open window and takes off.

The Crew heard what went on and are a bit freaked out. They don't know how badly hurt Hawk and George are. Jacques and the rest of the men can see that they're still a couple of blocks behind. They're very stressed that they can't get there faster. It should only take them another couple of minutes or so.

Although the gun had a silencer, as soon as the cabby heard the faint sound of gunfire, he hit the gas and raced out of there.

George got hit in the left shoulder and fell to the ground. The slug went right through the muscle, then hit the dump truck behind him. Hawk lucked out! The second bullet only ripped through the right sleeve of his coat, barely touching the skin. He'll only need a band aid. But, George is losing a fair amount of blood. Hawk picks up his buddy and walks him away from there.

He says, "Hey Georgie, when that shooter is far enough to stop to check the bag, he'll see the money isn't there. I'm pretty sure he's gonna come back looking for us. We need to get out of here, NOW!"

George tells Hawk, "See, my suspicions were right on, my friend. Druitt and the cop had a bad thing going!"

"Yeah man, you were right. We outsmarted them! But now, you're in trouble! Thank God he only hit you in the shoulder! You'll be okay, but I gotta get you to a hospital before you lose too much blood."

They walk around the corner onto 29th Street and go to a narrow alley between two buildings where they can get out of sight. This way, if the shooter does come back, he won't see them.

Hawk sees a cab, hails it down and tells the driver, "My friend just got shot by some punk and needs to get to a hospital right away! Where's the nearest hospital?"

The driver says, "Get in! St. Vincent Hospital on 34th Street isn't very far from here. We can get there in a few minutes."

Jacques and his men are less than a minute away. They heard everything and are doing their best to get to where the shooting took place. They're aware of the kind of injury George sustained and are confident he'll be okay. Still, they're very upset that it happened at all.

Sergio says, "I'm so glad Hawk accompanied him to the hospital instead of just putting him in a cab and taking off so he could go home."

Rick adds, "Hawk's a really good man. Despite his desperate need to get back home, he didn't abandon Georgie. He could be gone by now, but isn't. That says a lot about his character. He's the kind of guy anyone would be lucky to have for a friend."

Jacques also has a thought and says, "People like him are a rare commodity these days. A lesser man might have left George to fend for himself; not so with Hawk. That pleases me very much."

Chapter 23

The shooter returns

With what Hawk was overheard saying to George about the "shooter coming back," the Crew is pretty sure he will.

They check their scanner to pinpoint the cab carrying George and Hawk. The chase van with shadows Joe and Fritz are speeding toward them as they head to Saint Vincent Hospital.

Jacques radios them and says, "Get as close as possible to George once he's in the hospital, and find out whatever information you can on his condition."

The Crew and the other van with Chris and Paul arrive at the construction site. They were able to see its exact location on their scanner when the shooting happened.

Rick comes on the two-way, "Hey Chris and Paul, park next to that dump truck near the gate, with lights off and engine running. Be ready to move when you get the chance."

THE SHOOTER RETURNS

They wait for the right moment to strike. Only a few minutes go by before they spot a car doing a slow roll onto the work site with his lights off. He's taking his time scanning the area.

Paul radios in, "Boss, we have the car in our sights."

As the perp drives in and turns right to go the spot where he took Hawk's bag, Chris puts the van in gear and rams the front of his car. The airbags go off and dazes him, but he's not out. This gives Paul a chance to exit the van and get his gun ready for whatever comes next. His gun also has a silencer. The man struggles a bit to get out of his car, and when he's finally out, Paul can see that he's got a gun in his hand.

This adventure has now turned into a real drama! It's no longer just a surveillance game; it's time for extreme action!

As soon as Paul sees the guy raise his gun to shoot, he fires and hits him in the stomach. He drops the gun, grabs his gut and falls to his knees against the car. As he reaches for the gun a couple feet from him, Chris, now out of the van and standing over him, quickly kicks it away and picks it up.

In their ear piece, they're told by Jacques, "Find out who sent him!"

Paul kneels by the man's side and says, "Who sent you to do this?"

He doesn't want to say. He tells him, "If I tell you that, I'm a dead man! He'll kill me!"

"Tell me who it is and you'll be protected by a more powerful man than your boss, I assure you. Now then, who sent you?"

He says nothing.

On a hunch, Paul asks him, "Is it Captain Bates?"

Upon hearing that name, the perp's eyes open wide and Paul knows it's Bates.

To confirm that it is him, he says, "You're bleeding really bad and will die if we don't call an ambulance. Now then, tell me, is it Bates? Just nod your head if it is."

He nods. Paul and the Crew are sure they have the name of the man they need to bring to justice. The bullet probably tore through some vital organs. In the next minute, he passes out and slumps to the ground.

Paul, still squatting next to him, radios the Crew, "This guy may not make it. What do you propose we do?"

Jacques tells the driver, "Call 911 on Rick's cell phone. Tell them a man has been shot and lying on the ground at the construction site at 12th Avenue and West 29th." He continues, "That'll bring a couple of ambulances and a bunch of police cars to the scene. If he can be saved, at least we did our part."

He tells the men, "I'll bet Bates has him under his thumb, too. Maybe we can find out what he's got on him, later."

He'd like to have one of his men stay with him, but that would be too risky. Instead, he tells Paul and Chris. "Open the guy's car door and turn on his lights so the cops and medical team can see spot him easier."

He tells Chris, "Make sure you take his gun with you. We can't leave it for the cops. They'd be able to run a ballistics test. With this guy and George being shot around the same time frame, they just might put two and two together and come up with the idea of running a test to see if the slug they took out of George matches that gun. It would, and… we can't afford to have that happen. That'd really screw things up and put everything and everyone in jeopardy."

He pauses and says, "Hey Paul, get the man's wallet. I need his ID. I want to see if I'll need to compensate his family if he dies. God, I hope not! Even though this is a bad guy, it would still bother me very much that someone lost his life because of this adventure."

Paul takes his wallet, finds his driver's license and says to the Crew, "Gentlemen, the shooter's name is… Peter C. Taylor. Sergio clicks on and says, "Good job guys. Hold on to that wallet Paul, we'll get it from you later. Oh, and get that canvas bag in from his car. It's got those pamphlets in it. That would lead the cops back to Druitt's bank when they investigate this shooting, and to employees that saw who walked out with bags like that. It would most likely lead the detectives right to his door …can't have that! Now take off!"

Jacques is upset and puts the whole thing on himself. This was his idea, and now it had just gone south …two men shot.

Thinking back, the Crew figures the cabby was in on the scheme and was probably told to wait for George and Hawk to exit the bank; knowing the men would probably need a taxi. For now, they aren't worried about him. There'll be time to deal with him later if the need arises. Right now, the main concern is George's condition.

Jacques says, "It wasn't supposed to get this ugly! From now on, we need to make sure no one else gets hurt!"

No one says anything. Everyone heads for the hospital in a somber mood.

Chapter 24

At the hospital

Hawk is sitting in the guest waiting room while George is being attended to. He doesn't want to leave until he knows his friend will be okay. As he's sitting there, he's very conscious of the $100,000 he's carrying and makes sure none of it can fall out of his pockets, boots, or from inside his shirt. That's all he needs is for a $10,000 packet to hit the floor! After checking, he's confident that won't happen. Now, it's just a matter of sitting and waiting for the doctor to come out with the report on George.

As he waits to get word, he wonders where he'll sleep tonight. He thinks it through for a couple of minutes and figures that it shouldn't be a problem since has enough loose cash to get a room near the hospital.

POLICE INVESTIGATION

Every time someone is admitted to a hospital with a gunshot wound, the police are notified. If the patient is conscious, they want to come in and do an interview as soon as possible. While the doctors are working on George, a detective comes to the ER counter and asks about a shooting victim.

"Good evening nurse, I'm Detective Jim Gordon. I'm here to speak to a man that was brought in tonight with a gunshot wound. Where would I find him?"

The nurse says, "You must be talking about a Mr. Freeman, George Henry Freeman. He's in surgery as we speak and won't be able to speak to anyone until tomorrow morning. I expect that he'll be unconscious for several hours after he's out of the O.R. and will sleep through the night. If you come by around nine o'clock tomorrow, he should be awake and able to speak to you then."

"Boy, I really hate it when I make these trips for nothing!" says Gordon. "I should have called before coming in. Alright then, see you in the morning." He writes down George's name, thanks the nurse and leaves.

Hawk is sitting out of view near the reception desk and overheard the conversation. This is in his favor. He won't have to worry about having to answer any cop's questions tonight.

After over two hours in surgery, the surgeon comes out and asks for George's next of kin.

Hawk stands up and says, "I brought him in, doc. I'm the closest person he has right now."

He tells him, "We had a bit of a problem stopping the blood flow and had to do some tricky mending of his shoulder muscle. He's still under from the anesthesia and will be out for the night. You can see your friend in the morning. He's should be fine in a couple of weeks."

"Thanks doc. I'll be back tomorrow. Take good care of him for me! He's a good man. Oh, by the way, where can I find a cheap hotel close by?"

"Try the Even Hotel just north of here on 35th Street. That's about as cheap as you can get around here for a decent room."

Hawk repeats it, "Even Hotel 35th Avenue; got it." He starts walking toward the exit and says, "Thanks again doc. Much appreciated,"

He leaves the hospital at 10:30 pm. Shadow Fritz follows him while Joe stays to keep watch over George in whatever way he can. As he's walking on Eighth Avenue toward 35th Street, that $100,000 he's carrying makes him a bit paranoid. Now and then, he stops with his back against the buildings and looks around to see if anyone is tailing him. When he gets to 35th Street, he turns left at the corner and sees the hotel. That brings him relief. He goes in the hotel and asks for a room.

The clerk says, "I'll need to see a photo ID, and the room will cost you $145 for the night."

Hawk shows him his Ironworker photo ID and says, "My wallet was stolen by a pickpocket a few days ago. This is all I have for now."

The clerk says, "Okay, that'll have to do, but since you don't have a driver's license with an address on it, you'll have to pay

AT THE HOSPITAL

cash plus another $50 as security deposit. You'll get the fifty buck deposit back when you check out."

"I have cash," says Hawk.

The guy gives him an approving nod.

For the sake of not showing a large wad of bills, Hawk has already separated his money; $300 in his left pocket and $200 in small bills in his right. George told him to do that. This way, if he needed to pay for anything, people would only see him taking out two hundred dollars, and not all that he had.

He told Hawk, "Never, ever keep all your money in one pocket in this town. Split it up. Hide the largest amount well in your clothes somewhere. That's a smart street-guys' thing to do."

He pulls out the two hundred and hands it to the clerk.

The man gives him his change with the room key and says, "You'll be on the 3rd floor, room number 301. The elevator is down the hall on your right. Have a good night."

Again, the Crew heard all that just went on via the mic in Hawk's Saint Christopher medal. They're glad he made it there without any incident.

He goes to the elevator and heads up to the 3th floor. He's very tired and more than ready to settle in for the night. Once in the room, he gets all the money he has hidden on him and lays it out on the bed. He takes a long look at it and says to himself, "Diana and Jacob, this is for you. We're going to be alright from now on. Thank God! I can't wait to see you. I'm coming home!"

He undresses and goes to the bathroom to shower. After drying himself off and going back at the bed area, he looks at the cash he laid out and wonders what he should do with it for the night. He looks around the room for a good spot for it. He sees a plastic garbage bag lining the trash can and puts it inside. He places the bag under his pillow and puts his four inch folding knife in the open position on the night stand where he can get to it quickly. There shouldn't be any problem through the night, but this gives him peace of mind. He's never had to tuck away $100,000 for the night before. This is a whole new experience. With his loot nice and secure under his head, knife at the ready, he's fast asleep within ten minutes.

Fritz radios the Crew to say, "Hawk is tucked in for the night." His Saint Christopher medal is still sending out a beacon and audio. The men will be monitoring him on their scanners.

As for George, he's safe and sound, but just the same, shadow Joe will be around in case something comes up. The hospital staff removed George's medal when he went to X-Ray and then to surgery. They put it in a bag with the rest of his belongings. The scanner shows its location as Recovery Room number 4 on the 2nd floor. The Crew knows they'll need to get a "bug" in there. Joe will handle it.

The van with the Crew is parked near the hospital. Sergio goes to the Emergency Room desk to inquire about George's condition. He tells them that he's Mr. Yacone, director of the homeless shelter where George is a volunteer.

The nurse tells him, "I can only tell you the same thing I told a detective that came by to talk to him earlier; he's in a recovery room and can't receive any visitor until tomorrow. Besides, it's way past visiting hours. Sorry, hospital rules."

Mr. Yacone gives the nurse his cell number and tells her to call him if anything comes up during the night. She places the number in George's folder with a note directing the doctors to call him.

As he's leaving, he sees Joe at the far end of the waiting room and radios him via his sleeve mic. "Glad you're here, Joe. Let us know if anything comes up. Have a good night."

"You got it Mr. Malich. Have a good night, sir. By the way, I'll be staying near George in a storage room for the night where there are a lot of spare mattresses. I'll be comfortable enough. I want to make sure I'm close by."

Malich clicks back, "Good man, Joe. Don't know what we'd do without you."

Hot News

Sergio makes his way out the door and into one of the vans. As he settles into one of the nice soft seats, Jacques tells him that while he was checking on George's status, he got a call from a friend at headquarters who told him what a confidante told him.

"There was a rumor that Druitt was involved in a very bad hit and run accident in Captain Bates' district three years ago. As the story goes, Druitt left a party quite drunk and struck a fifty-three year old man. He suffered severe injuries. One of those injuries was the loss of part of his right leg. The car was damaged and Bates had it taken away to be torched. He drove Druitt back to the party he was at, then told him to call 911 to say that his car was stolen. Nothing ever came of it."

He continues, "There you have it gentlemen, Bates has Druitt by the 'you know what' and is manipulating him. It's time to burn this guy. We did indeed get an adventure going, but at the same time, we may just be the Crew that will free Druitt and end Bates' crooked schemes. I'll do some more follow up on this and see where it leads."

LAMENTING OVER MISHAPS

The third day of this adventure surely hasn't gone as planned. Hawk isn't on his way home and George is in a hospital bed with a gunshot wound. To make things even worse, the shooter, Pete Taylor didn't make it. He bled out and is now in the morgue. Jacques got word about that through his sergeant buddy, and feels terrible about it.

Trying to take away some of the guilt he feels, Rick tells him, "Jacques, don't beat yourself up over this! Remember, Taylor shot George and Hawk. They could both be dead! He was going to shoot Paul and Chris, and they too could both be dead! There was no other way to handle this. This was a bad guy. Paul saved himself and Chris. Think of it that, my friend."

"You're right, Rick. Having lived a life that is so far removed from this kind of down and dirty street stuff just shocks my sensibilities. One needs to have thick skin to handle this sort of thing. I can appreciate what the 'men in blue' have to endure in this city. I suppose all that's happened so far in this adventure is a good lesson in the 'realities of life.' Well, enough of that. Right now, I need to put Peter Taylor behind me and focus on George."

CHAPTER 25

DETECTIVE GORDON

The next day at 9 am as George lays there sipping orange juice through a straw, a man in a suit walks in and introduces himself as Detective James Gordon. Of course he's comes to talk to him about the shooting.

Gordon starts off with the obvious question…

"Mr. Freeman, can you tell me what happened and where?"

So as to not put himself too near the place where he was shot, he tells Gordon.

"Well, as you can see, I was shot in the shoulder. As best I can remember, we were on 12th Avenue somewhere between West 32nd or 33rd streets around seven-thirty or eight when it happened."

"You said, we.., who else was with you?"

"Oh, that'd be Fred. We're both homeless and were on our way to catch a bus to go to a men's shelter on East 30th Street."

"Why did the guy shoot you? Was there some sort of altercation?"

"No, no altercation. It was bizarre, man. I accidently bumped into some guy as he walked by us, and he went crazy! I mean… out of his mind crazy! You know what I mean? Anyway, I just bumped him a little! I apologized, but the guy went on cussing me out, pulled out a gun and shot at us! I got the worst of it. Fred was lucky. The bullet went through his coat sleeve and slightly nicked his right arm!"

"Can you give me a description of the shooter?"

"Some white guy about five foot ten, two hundred pounds, maybe. He had a scraggly beard and wore a black hoody. I can't really give you any details of his face. It was getting dark and everything happened so fast. After he shot at us, he took off running. Fred picked me up, hailed down a cab, put me in it and brought me here. That's about it, detective."

As Gordon scribbles down the little bit of information he got, George asks, "Hey, what are the chances of finding this moron?"

"We'll Mr. Freeman, I'd love to say we'll find him, but frankly the chances are slim to none. I don't have a lot to go on here."

"That's what I figured. What a City! Great luck I have; broke, homeless and shot!"

"Yeah! What a city. This happens way too often. As a matter of fact, another man was also shot not too far from where you were shot. I'm just wondering if it's the same guy who shot you. It could very well be. Anyway, we just keep doing what we can do to catch perps like him, but it's not easy. By the way, do you know where Fred is right now? I'd like to talk to him. Maybe there's something he could tell me that would help."

"No I don't. I only met him a few days ago. He told me yesterday that he'd be leaving early today for the Watertown area where he came from. He hates this city. I figure he's already gone by now."

"Okay, thanks for your time Mr. Freeman."

"Let me know if you get anything on the guy who shot me, okay?"

"I'll let you know if anything shakes out George. Take care!"

"I will. And you too, detective. Watch out for the crazies out there."

Gordon winks at him, flips the cover on his note pad and walks out of the room.

Joe, who's been watching over Georgie, tells the Crew, "Gentlemen, the cop is gone and George is resting nicely. Oh, and while he was being operated on last night, I figured I'd need to get close to him afterward and managed to score a stethoscope and a doctor's white lab coat. You can call me Dr. Guiniache. I was able to blend in and placed a bug in his room around midnight. Were you able to hear what he and the cop talked about?"

Jacques comes back, "Yes we did! George played dumb. He didn't give the detective anything that would prompt him to follow up. We're good for now, but be ready for anything. Remember, Bates is still a major factor in this equation. I suspect he heard about the shooting. I'm sure he got word that the officers on the scene searched the car and saw that it was registered to Pete Taylor. Oh yeah, there was no mention of any canvas bag found in the car.

As far as Bates knows …either George or Hawk shot his guy, and Hawk still has the money. Right now, we have to figure he checked the local hospitals and found out George was brought in…and is still alive. He'll be safe for now. Bates knows he doesn't have his money with him, but Hawk on the other hand, is still going to be his prime target. He's probably hoping he'll show up at the hospital to see George, and when that happens, one of his men will be looking to get his money."

Chapter 26

Hawk visits George

Earlier on, while George was still resting in the hospital, before he had his chat with Detective Gordon, Hawk got up at 7:45, shaved, got dressed, and put the money in his clothes and boots like he did the day before. He went down to the front desk to check out; turned in his key, got his $50 deposit back, and then, went to the hotel restaurant to get some breakfast. He finished eating around 9:15 and headed out to the hospital. He wants to see that George is okay and to tell him that he needs to be on his way.

He arrives in about twenty-five minutes and needs to find out which room George is in. But, just in case one of Bates' guys is there waiting for him to show up, he uses the hospital phone in the lobby and asks the receptionist for the room number.

She tells Hawk, "Mr. Freeman was transferred from the recovery room early this morning. He's on the 5th floor, room 11."

Jacques' man Joe, who is still watching out for George, has Hawk in sight. The hallway is very busy with staff and visitors.

Hawk finds room 11 and goes in. He's relieved that it's a single-patient room. This will allow them to talk privately. He sees his partner on the bed with his eyes closed; approaches him quietly, and taps his foot. George opens his eyes, smiles at Hawk and shakes his extended hand. They have the following conversation…

"Hey Cochise, it's really good seeing you, man! Sit down."

"Good to see you too, pale face."

George asks, "So, how was your night; were you able to find a good place to sleep?"

"I slept pretty well. I found a room in a hotel just a couple of blocks from here. Man, that pocket money I had on me sure came in handy. Since I didn't have a credit card or a driver's license, the clerk would only take cash. But, forget that, how are you feeling, man?"

"I hurt like hell, but I'll be okay. Hey, I need to tell you that a detective was here. As far as he knows, your name is Fred. That's what I told him. He doesn't have a clue as to what really happened. He'll probably figure this is one of those unsolvable crimes and just let it slide. They have tons of rape and murder cases to deal with. Me being one of dozens of people getting shot, but still alive, and no suspect captured, I'm sure it won't take priority over the more pressing cases they have."

Hawk says, "Did he ask how we knew each other and where we were going at the time of the shooting?"

"I told him that we only met a few days ago and were on our way to the men's shelter on East 30th when some nut shot us because I bumped into him, and you brought me here by cab.

That's all you need to say if you're ever questioned. Oh, and one more thing, I gave him a phony description of the guy who shot us; some white guy about five foot ten, two hundred pounds, scraggly beard and wearing a black hoody. And, when he asks where you could be found so he could question you, I told him that you were already on your way to the Watertown area. You got all that?"

"Got it, I'm Fred…punk shot us because you bumped into him. But, I don't plan on talking to any cops, my friend."

"I figured you didn't. So what are you going to do now, Hawk?"

"You know I gotta get home, man. I was ready yesterday when we left the bank, then all hell broke loose! I should be in Buffalo by now, but I couldn't leave without seeing you. You gonna be okay if I split?"

"I'll be fine! I appreciate you coming in, buddy. I knew you would. Now, take off! Get back to your wife and kid and enjoy your dough! Start a new life, man! There's nothing else you can do here. Just be careful when you make your way to the bus station."

"I will, don't worry. I'll be sure to keep an eye out for any suspicious characters. I should be fine."

"One more thing, take the canvas bag Druitt gave me. It's over there on the chair. Fill it with anything worthless and use it as a decoy. When you travel, make like you're holding onto it like it's priceless. If anyone goes for anything you have, it'll be that. Now, get yourself to the terminal! Go home!"

"Thanks for seeing me through this, George. Without you, things would have turned out a lot differently. I owe you one!"

"You owe me nothing. Take good care of yourself, and godspeed."

Hawk hands him a slip of paper with his address and phone number on it and says, "If you're ever in the Buffalo area, I'd love to see you and hear how you're doing."

"You got it, Cochise. You may just see me pop in one day. I'd love to meet your wife and son …and your friends. Hey! Wouldn't we have a great story to tell them?"

"Yes we would pale face, yes we would."

"Alright Hawk, get out of here! Go man! Get back to Buffalo where you belong!"

Hawk shakes his hand and tells him, "So long Georgie. I'll never forget you, man. You're the best."

CHAPTER 27

HAWK AT THE BUS TERMINAL

As Hawk leaves the hospital, he's spotted getting in a cab by one of the men the captain posted there. He phones Bates to let him know Hawk is on the move and that he's tailing him. Shadows Chris and Paul see what's going on and follow him. The good thing about this is that they're a step ahead of everything Hawk's pursuer is doing.

Everyone arrives at the bus terminal around 11:30 am. Hawk goes to the counter and buys a ticket. He's all set. All he needs to do now is wait to hear… *"Attention, the bus for Buffalo is now boarding passengers."* It'll be leaving at 1:30.

While he's waiting and without being too obvious, he casually puts his hand inside his coat breast pocket to check the $40,000 he placed there. He does the same for the other $40,000 in his calf-high engineer boots ($20,000 in each boot), and $19,500 in two packs inside his shirt just above his belt. Knowing that his money is secure, he gets as comfortable as he can and waits for the announcement. As per George's suggestion, he's holding on tight to the canvas bank bag he gave him to use as a decoy.

Bates' man sees that and calls his boss to say, "Hawk has the money in a bag and is holding onto it as if his life depended on it."

The captain replies, "Alright then! Find the right opportunity to snatch it from him and get out of the terminal as fast as you can. It's got to be done before he boards that bus! Once he's aboard, he's gone…and so is the hundred grand!"

At 1:15 pm, the announcement is made that the bus for Buffalo will be leaving in 15 minutes. Hawk's heart jumps with joy knowing that he's finally on his way. He's seventh in line to board. His pursuer stands close to him waiting for the chance to grab the bag. He has it slung over his shoulder and as he relaxes his grip on it while he goes in his side coat pocket to get some gum, Bates' guy moves in with a knife, cuts the shoulder strap, grabs the bag and gets lost in the crowd. The bus driver sees what just happened and yells for him to stop.

Hawk tells him, "Don't worry about it. It's an old bag with nothing of value in it. Besides, it's much more important that I get home tonight than to worry about the few worthless items I have in there. I don't have time for the cops get involved and answer questions that will make me miss my ride home."

He thanks him for being concerned and gets on the bus. Like George's "Plan B" at the bank, he figured he'd do the same thing by finding old magazines at the hospital that gave the approximate weight the cash would weigh, and put them in the bag. He also picked up a roll of duct tape at the terminal to wrap around it to make it look more secure. This gave the thief even more reason to believe he got what he went after. As far he knows, he's got the loot.

Being in the terminal with security cameras all over, the thief knows he can't stop to look inside. He keeps moving as fast as he can, makes it outside the terminal and heads for his car that's parked two blocks away. It'll be a little while before he can get there and cut the tape around the bag to get a peek inside. By then, Hawk and his money will be gone.

With the bus on its way, Hawk sits back and can completely relax for the first time in three days. He's finally heading back to his wife and son…five hundred miles away.

In the meantime, Chris and Paul, who followed Bates' man outside the bus terminal, are very close behind. Two other shadows, Max and Tony, are following in a van in order to assist them when they nab the thief. As the bad guy nears his car, Chris is closest and zaps him with a stun gun. Down he goes. The van rolls up to their location, they load in their bad guy and head out. All four men involved in this chase are in the van; Max is driving. Tony and Paul tie up their prize and place a hood over his head. They're taking him to a vacant building by the river that Sergio owns.

Meanwhile, Captain Bates sent one of his uniform officers to the hospital to speak to George and get as much information about the shooting to see if there's anything that will connect him to it. As the officer asks about the patient, he's told by the hospital staff that he was already questioned by a detective and that there were strict orders to not allow anyone else to question him. He calls the captain and gives him the news. Bates tells him to get back to the job of patrolling his beat, that right now, George is not his main concern. At this point, Bates doesn't know the attempt to take Hawk's money has failed and that his man has been abducted. This puts the Crew ahead in the game and buys them time for their next move.

CHAPTER 28

ROBERT GREENE'S INTERROGATION

Hawk's bus is now on the expressway heading west out of the city toward the I-90 and on to Buffalo. Every mile going in that direction brings him closer to his family. He's very much at ease and runs all sorts of thoughts through his head. He spends some time figuring out what he'll do with the small fortune he has. No definite plans, but he knows for sure that it's going to change his life in many good ways.

While the bus is taking him home, back in the city at 2:30 in the afternoon, the Crew and some of the shadows have gathered in the warehouse to interrogate their catch from the bus terminal. Rick starts by asking him his name. He doesn't answer.

Shadow Fritz folds him over in the chair they've put him in and takes his wallet from his back pocket. He pulls out his driver's license and says, "Boss, according to this, he's Robert Xavier Greene, twenty-six years old."

Jacques steps in and says, "Robert, I have one question for you and you'd do well to provide us with the right answer! All we want to know is…who sent you to go after the man at the terminal?"

They can hear him breathing hard, like a man who is very scared. He doesn't seem to be a real hard case, just some young guy who got himself into something really bad.

He says, "If I tell you, will you let me go?"

"In time, we will let you go." Jacques says. "But, you need to get real with us and give up the name of the man who sent you! So…who sent you?"

He tells them that it was Captain Bates from the north precinct. He also tells them that if he failed the mission of grabbing the money bag that he would be in a world of trouble.

He breaks down crying and says, "I have a wife and two kids. I'm on parole and if I don't come back with the money, Bates said he'd make sure I'd go back to jail and serve out the rest of my sentence. That's another two and a half years! I can't go back in there. I just can't! My wife would leave me."

Rick asks him, "What were you in jail for?"

"It was for cocaine and heroin possession with intent to sell. They gave me three to five years in jail. Since it was my first arrest and I have a family, I served two and a half and was paroled. If I mess up, they'll put me back in to serve the rest of the sentence and more time for any other crime I commit. I can't do more jail time, I'd rather die!"

Jacques tells him, "Okay! We have the name, but you know we can't let you go just yet. You'll remain here until we deal with the captain. We need to make sure Bates leaves you alone. Once we do that, we'll let you get back to your family. By the way, do you have a regular job?"

He tells him, "Yes, I drive trucks for RDS Delivery Service on 11th Street."

"That's good!" says Jacques, "Now, you need to call your wife and tell her your company is sending you to Rochester to pick up an important shipment and that you'll be gone a couple of days, maybe three. What's your home phone number?"

He gives them the number; Rick dials it on Robert's own cell phone, puts it in his hand and tells him to make it short and sweet. His wife Sherrie answers. He tells her that he'll be on a road trip to Rochester for a few days to pick up an important shipment and that he should be back in a couple of days.

After that, Rich says, "Hey, the captain will be wondering where he and the money is. Robert needs to get in touch with him right away to tell him something that will buy us some time so we can get to him, but what?"

"I've got it." says Jacques. "Robert, although you did get the bag from Hawk, you'll call the captain and tell him that you weren't able to get close enough to Hawk to get the money because there were too many people around him. Also, tell him that your boss at the trucking company called you to go to a Jersey plant to pick up a very important shipment by six and that you won't be back until nine tonight."

Robert calls Bates and tells him exactly what Jacques just told him to say.

Bates is fuming. He's scary angry with him and says, "You blew the assignment! You IDIOT! You just cost me a hundred grand! I want you to meet me at the Onyx Bar tonight at nine. You better be there! Don't make me chase you, Robert! If you do, I'll make things twice as bad for you!"

With fear in his voice, Robert tells him, "Captain, I'm really sorry! I didn't mean to fail you. It just wasn't possible to get the bag from such a big guy. Please don't send me back to jail!"

"We'll talk about that when I see you at the Onyx. Just make sure you're on time…nine o'clock! BE THERE!" Robert can hear Bates slam down the receiver.

After hanging up, Jacques tells him he needs to call his boss at the truck company and tell him that he's down with a bad case of the flu and won't be in for the next two to three days. This will be a good cover for his absence for a few days while they take care of Bates.

Rick dials the number and Robert tells his boss and pretty much tells him what Jacques told him to say. With that done, he's taken to another section of the building. He's locked in an eight by ten room with only a small window about ten feet up that is open to let in fresh air. There's no way for him to get up there and escape. They place a fan in the room to circulate the air. He's told to not remove the hood until he hears the door close.

When the two men who put him there reach the door, one of them turns off the light and tells him he's free to take off the hood. As he hears the door shut, he rips it off. There's only a small light in there. He looks around and sees a cot and a camping type toilet he can use. On a small table, he finds a gallon of water, a glass and some snack food. He sits on the cot and listens to the muffled conversation in a room about a hundred feet from where he is, but can't make out anything that's being said. He lies down and resigns himself to the fact that he's a prisoner and will be there for a while.

Chapter 29

Jacques meets with Druitt

The conversation that's going on in the other room is about Druitt. Jacques tells everybody that he'll be going to the City Businessmen's Bank to confront his banker friend to see what's going on. He wants to find out if he'll come clean. If he does, he'll figure a way to help him get Captain Bates off his back. It's now 3 pm. He calls Druitt and tells him that he needs to see him right away.

He arrives at the bank at 3:15 and makes his way to Druitt's office. He brought along a tape recorder so he can record their conversation. As soon as he enters, he can see that Druitt is uneasy. He comes right to the point and tells him that he knows Bates has something on him, and that he cooked up a scheme to relieve Hawk and George of their money once they left the bank.

Jacques meets with Druitt

He says to him in a chastising tone, "That little scheme you two cooked up got George shot! ...and I'm pretty angry about it!"

Before Jacques can say another word, Druitt says, "Jacques, I'm so, so sorry George got shot. I feared something like this was going to happen eventually. And, you are right about Captain Bates, he does have something on me. It has to do with a hit and run situation I was involved in three years ago. I was drunk and hit a man, then took off. One of Bates' officers saw it and gave chase. When I was stopped, I was about a mile away from the scene of the accident. The captain was called in and when he arrived, he was told that I was manager of the City Businessmen's Bank. He spoke to me privately and promised to withhold the police report from the courts and from my superiors if I helped him do something. Part of that 'something' was what happened to Hawk and George. If the bank's Board of Trustees ever found out, I would be fired and could go to jail! Can you imagine me in jail? I don't know what to do, Jacques! The man I hit ended up in a coma for two months due to head trauma, lost his right leg below the knee and has ongoing back problems. His name is Miles Nevels. There isn't a day that goes by that I don't ask God for forgiveness!"

Jacques doesn't let on that he knows about the hit and run accident. He says to him, "Okay Dex, relax! I'm your friend. Your secret is safe with me. You know you need to do something for that man, right?"

"I've already done that by sending him $200 a week as a way to compensate him. So far, he's received close to $32,000. In a letter of apology, I let him know that it's from the man who hit him, and that he can expect money every week."

Jacques says, "That's good Dex, $800 a month. Keep doing that as long as you can!"

"I will," says Druitt.

"Now look, I'm here to help you and to make sure both you and George are safe from Bates and his crew. When you said, *'I feared something like this was going to happen eventually,'* what did you mean by that?"

"I'm so ashamed Jacques, but I have to get this off my chest. Bates pressured me to let him know when wealthy customers made large withdrawals. For the sake of bank records, I as manager, always sign off on all large amounts leaving this bank. He made me give him names and addresses. You may have heard news stories on TV that reported this person or that person was robbed at home. Each robbery resulted in the thieves netting anywhere from $250,000, to $500,000 from rich folks who use cash for gambling, private deals, or whatever."

He hesitates a bit and then says, "Jacques, I believe one of the people robbed was an employee of an extremely powerful man in the city. I have a few rich and powerful clients who bank here and I can't be positive as to which one was robbed. But, I know this much, whoever it was must surely want to find out who did it. I have no idea how much he lost. Whatever the amount, you know he wants it back! For people like him, I can't sign off because they keep their cash in safe deposit boxes. From time to time, they have one of their guys comes in, go to the deposit box with a briefcase and do whatever they need to do, then leave. It could be a deposit or a withdrawal, I don't know. At any rate, Bates got one of the big guys' money."

As the two men continue talking, Jacques finds out the captain has a crew of released felons doing the dirty work. Druitt has some idea how much money his thieves have stolen so far. He thinks that it could be a couple of million dollars. Bates told him that he has almost enough money put away to retire at the end of this summer. He tells Jacques that it wasn't a random score the day they hit one of the big guys.

"He says, "Somehow, Bates knew one of them was coming to take out a large sum. His guys were waiting. One of them put a gun to his back as soon as he came out of the bank, walked him to a waiting van, pushed him inside, and took off!"

Jacques says, "That rat is more than dirty! Thanks for all the info. It helps a lot. It gives me an idea how we can straighten out the whole thing. Okay Dex, I want you to set up a meeting today at 5:30PM with Bates. Tell him it's extremely important that you two meet. I'll need to use the office next to yours to make a couple of phone calls."

It's now 4:30. Jacques goes to the adjoining office and calls shadow Max to meet at the bank with a "wire." The plan is to wire Druitt so they'll be able to hear and record his meeting with the captain.

He also calls a sergeant friend of his at the north precinct to inquire about Bates. His name is Frank. He tells Jacques that Bates is a dirty cop with quite a bit of muscle and connection, and that he's gotten rid of several good officers who wouldn't bow down to him. He asks where he might find the Captain when he's outside his home; restaurants, bars, massage parlor or off-track betting.

His buddy tells him, "He usually goes to a small bar called the Onyx Pub on 130th Street. It's run by Mickey Sperduti. He meets up with some of his non-cop buddies. Some of those guys look a bit shady, if you know what I mean."

Jacques thanks him, hangs up and places a call to Rick and Sergio to tell them to get a crew ready to go for tonight; to capture Bates.

CHAPTER 30

DRUITT MEETS WITH BATES

It's close to 5:30. The guys are in the van and monitoring Druitt's conversation. So far, he's only spoken to his secretary, a few staff people and customers. Jacques' men are watching for Bates' arrival. He's right on time.

Bates walks into the bank and heads for Druitt's office, and in his usual gruff voice he says, "So what is it you needed to talk to me about Dexter?"

Druitt says, "Two things. First, I got a call from George this morning telling me that he'll be coming to get his money tomorrow around 3 pm. And secondly, I don't want to do this anymore. I won't give you any more leads on customers taking out large cash amounts! You've got me in way too deep! I can't take it anymore! You need to leave me alone! I need my life back! You've gotten a lot of money from my customers. This needs to end!"

"Yeah...I got a lot of money from past heists, but guess what? ...yesterday's score was a complete flop! George didn't take his money out and Hawk got away with all of his. He made it out of town with every bit of it!

You say you want your life back, eh Bozo? You don't quit till I say you quit! You got that?! Since yesterday was a bust, to make up for what I lost, I expect you to provide me with a couple of your customers when they make a large withdrawal. Do you understand me? Or, I can release the 'hit and run' information to your boss! I know you don't want that. Now then, I have to get ready to set George up for his big let-down. You just mind the store! I'll take care of the rest."

The meeting took about twenty minutes. Bates leaves the bank. The crew in the van has his entire conversation on tape with Druitt. Now, they need to plan how they'll snag the captain. He's heading for the precinct to take care of some department business. Shadow Max follows him and parks outside the station waiting for the moment when he leaves so he can radio in and tell the others to get the crew ready.

By 7:45 pm, Bates is done with his work. He tells the desk sergeant that he'll be at the Onyx Pub if he's needed for anything, and exits the station. Max lets the guys know and they get moving. Shadows Paul and Chris will do the honors for this pick up. Rick wants to be in on the action and boards the van.

Max follows Bates, and in about twenty minutes, he sees the Pub. He tells the Crew their man has arrived. Once they reach the place and park, Rick enters in disguise and sits at the end of the bar so he can see all the players. He sees the captain drinking

Druitt meets with Bates

with a few of his cohorts, chatting and laughing at some dumb stories. He sets up his cell phone on "camera" so the guys watching on a monitor can see what's going on.

It's getting close to nine o'clock, the time Robert is supposed to show up. He can see the captain is looking very perturbed as he keeps looking toward the door at everyone walking in. He's hoping to see Robert pop in, but when he sees that it's 9:10, he knows the kid isn't going to show.

Rick notices Bates getting up to leave and tells the men outside to get ready for him. He goes to the parking lot, and as he nears his car, they zap him with a stun gun. The next thing he knows, he's in a van with a hood over his head and handcuffed with his own cuffs. They drive to their "holding center" and the men bring him to the same room Robert was brought to for questioning. As with Robert, they keep the hood in place. None of the men can afford to be seen.

Jacques starts the interrogation. "Captain, we know you've been involved in some heavy duty criminal activity with Druitt at the Businessmen's Finance Bank, and recently, you and your men have been chasing down two men who took money out. We know your little band of thieves have robbed a few people who've made large withdrawals from the same bank. My question to you is… how much of that money do you have and where is it?"

Bates wants to know who these guys are and says, "Are you guys Federal Agents or something? Just who the hell are you?"

Sergio says, "We're not the Feds. We're a whole different kind of law people. You might say we're… agents for regular folks."

Bates tries to be a tough guy and says in an authoritative voice, "If you're not real law enforcement people, you're in serious trouble? You can't grab a New York City police captain and do this to him. That's imprisonment and kidnapping! Have you ANY idea what kind of trouble you just got yourself into by doing this?!"

Rick comes back with, "Yes, we know exactly who we're messing with… we can, and have, grabbed a New York City police captain. Imprisonment and kidnapping a crook is nothing compared to what you've been doing for the past three years. Yeah! We know about you ripping off good folks. We're not in trouble! YOU are, Bates!"

He shouts out, "Look! We can make a deal here, guys! I'll split the money with you!"

Jacques tells him, "Oh, we'll get the money alright, and you WILL leave Druitt alone. You see, we know who you are, where you work and live and what you've been up to. You have NO bargaining chips. We have them all…Bozo!"

As soon as he hears the word "Bozo," he knows he was set up, that they wired Druitt. He realizes that he's done for and tells them that if he's released, he'll make everything right again by returning the money to the people he stole from, and vows to destroy the report he has on Druitt.

Rick, Sergio and Jacques step out of the room and Jacques says to them, "Letting him go is not an option. Who knows what he might be able to do with his gang of thieves? We can't cut him loose. We have to figure out a way to get to his money and the

DRUITT MEETS WITH BATES

police report he has on Druitt. Let's get back in there and find out where the money and the report on Druitt are."

Sergio says to Bates, "We can't let you go until we know where the money is, and also, the police report you have on Druitt. If you won't give us that information, then we'll make you wish your mother never bore you! You have no option. It's tell us what we need to know or get ready for the worst time of you miserable life! What do you say?"

Bates sits there quietly for a moment processing all he's just been told. Finally, he says, "Okay! Okay! The money is in the Knox Bank on Lexington and Martin Luther King Boulevard. The problem is…you can't get to it without me. Everything is in a safe deposit box. I'm the only one who can get to it. That means you have to let me out of here if you want to get your hands on it. And, as for Druitt's police report… well gentlemen, that's in my office at the precinct in a locked file. You can't get in there either. It seems to me that you have a huge dilemma, wouldn't you say?"

Jacques smiles, then fires back, "You dumb ass, delusional, tub of lard! …you want to play games?! Now it's my turn! You don't know who YOU'RE dealing with! I'll have you know that I am a personal friend with bank manager Arnold Ferro at Knox Bank and can have him open up your precious safe deposit box for me. You are done! So, you will be our guest for a few days until I get ALL your money. Oh by the way, I have friends at your precinct that will help me get Druitt's police report. I have people who can open up any locked cabinet or vault. Checkmate! …BOZO!"

As the saying goes, Bates *"doesn't know whether to s--t or go blind."* He bows his head and says no more. He becomes like any other defeated man who has just realized he's become powerless. He's quiet and submissive. The men lead him out and put him in a secured room in another part of the warehouse, away from Robert.

Back in the interrogation area, Sergio thinks outside the box a bit and tells Jacques he needs to call his friend at the precinct to tell everybody there that Bates called in to say he's sick and won't be in for a few days. That'll cover his absence. That way, no red flags for Bates not being around. Jacques agrees.

Jacques calls his police friend Frank at home and tells him that he has Bates in a lockup and that he needs to get into his office tomorrow to get something from his personal file cabinet. Franks is glad he's got the captain and tells him that the best time to do what he plans will be around 6 am.

It's all set. Jacques has a top notch locksmith in mind that opened one of his malfunctioning safes. He trusts him completely. On several other occasions, he's opened safes on the sly for special clients who needed to get their hands on very important documents. Frank tells Jacques that he'll put the word out tomorrow at the precinct about the captain being out for a few days. That will allow him time to do what he needs to do.

CHAPTER 31

HAWK'S DILEMMA

While the Crew and shadows were busy bagging Bates and interrogating him, miles away, Hawk's trip got interrupted. Although it's early spring, snow storms are always a possibility this time of year in New York; especially for Buffalo, Rochester, and Syracuse. The Great Lakes can produce snow falls right into the month of May.

Earlier in the day, at around 6:30 pm, as Hawk's bus rolled along the I-90, it ran right into a freak storm and the driver was forced to pull into a service stop just a bit west of Syracuse. The passengers were told they'd need to hold up inside the service building until it would be safe to travel again. According to news reports, the storm was supposed to let up around 9:30 or 10 pm. Hawk went inside the facility, bought a coffee and found a booth in the restaurant area where he could wait it out.

At eight o'clock, he realized he needed to call his friend's house in Irving and give him a status report. He told him to let his wife know that he was on his way home and would contact him as soon as he got to the Buffalo Ellicott Street bus station around three or four in the morning, if the weather cooperated.

After hanging up, he got another cup of coffee and found another seat where he could relax and read a newspaper that he bought in the facility's store. A half hour later, that second cup of coffee necessitated a visit to the men's room. He entered a stall and as he loosened his belt, a $10,000 pack of money fell out from inside his shirt. A man in the next stall saw Hawk snatch it up. He hoped the guy didn't see it. As he flushed the toilet when he was done, he could hear the guy next door hurrying to get out. That set off an alarm in his head. He figured he saw the money when it hit the floor and could very well be looking to relieve him of it. Hawk thought about the possibility that he might have a friend out there to help him do it. He really didn't know what to do next. His problem was that the man would be able to see him exit the stall and would know what he looked like. Hawk, on the other hand, wouldn't have any idea who to look for. He needed to be very sharp.

He secured his money and exited his stall. As he walked toward the sinks, he saw a guy washing his hands and looking into the mirror in a way that allowed him to observe the people coming out of the stalls. Hawk had his number. He had the look of a sleaze-ball; the kind of guy that hangs around places like this for a chance to steal anything of value from careless travelers. The game now became …who can outsmart the other? Hawk is a man of the streets and knew that he'd probably have to deal with this mutt!

He returned to the cafeteria and checked the time, it was 8:35. He went to a seat where he could have his back to the wall and have a view of the entire area…and the creep. He knew there were security cameras throughout the facility and he'd have to be very careful how he handled this problem. He couldn't get caught looking like he was doing anything wrong! As he scanned the room to find the perp, he spotted him peering behind a display in the souvenir shop. Keeping his head fairly straight, he used his peripheral vision to keep the guy in his sights. He saw him browsing through a book and doing quick glances at him about every ten seconds or so. This went on for about twenty minutes.

Hawk knew the man couldn't rob him in the service center and would have to wait till he got outside. The guy probably figured that when Hawk left, it would be to go to his car and that's when he'd strike. Of course, he would eventually see his target boarding a bus and he'd have no opportunity of robbing him. Hawk thought about all that and was pretty sure he'd make it back on the bus without being mugged. Still, he thought that this monkey could be desperate enough to try something. Another thought crossed his mind, "Does this guy have a gun, a knife, or a friend with a gun or a knife, waiting to join him in the robbery?" There was no way of knowing.

By 8:55 pm the storm seemed to have subsided some but not enough for the bus to continue on to Buffalo. The temperature outside was about twenty-five degrees and the snow was swirling around, making for poor visibility.

Hawk turned toward a window to make it look like he was looking at the storm. The combination of the darkness outside and the light inside made the glass a perfect mirror for him to watch the guy. He could see him clearly. He took out a pack of cigarettes, turned and walked toward the doors. The man followed and watched which way he turned. He saw him going left, and then made another left to the dark side of the building. Hawk tucked himself deep into a recessed doorway and waited to see if the character followed him. It was very dark back there and he was practically invisible. It wasn't long before his pursuer walked to the side of the building and passed right by him. He stopped very close to where Hawk was hidden. He looked to the left and to the right, then looked back toward the main entrance in case he missed him doubling back somehow. As he turned back the other way, Hawk moved in and hammered him with a solid punch to the side of the jaw and knocked him out cold.

He did a quick body search to see if he had a weapon. Sure enough, he was packing a "Saturday night special." It was a little .22 caliber pistol. Although Hawk is a big guy, there was no doubt that gun would have been enough to kill him. He threw it as far as he could into a snow-covered ditch; he wanted no part of it.

He searched the guy for car keys, found them and thought to himself, *Hey, I could take his car and head on out of here.* But then reasoned, *If I take it, when this jerk wakes up, he'll call the cops and tell them what kind of car to look for. That's too risky.*

He put the keys back in the punk's pocket and left him. For the time being, the would-be robber was unconscious but would wake up soon enough. Hawk didn't want to be around when that happened. He needed to get away from there quick, but what could he do? The bus wouldn't move for another couple of hours or so.

Getting a ride home

He went out to the parking area, saw tractor trailers lined up in the trucker's service area, ready to head west. He eyed a Kaplan Trucking Company rig loaded with steel beams and wondered if that could be his ride to the Buffalo area. As he approached the truck, the driver saw Hawk motioning for him to roll down his window.

He rolled it down and asked, "What's up, pal? I was just about to hit the road. What do you need?"

With great urgency in his voice, Hawk said, "Man, I hope you can help me! The bus I was on limped into this service stop and needs one of their specialized mechanics to come in and fix it. They said they'd send another bus so we could continue, but it won't be here for another four or five hours. I can't afford to lose that much time! I desperately need to get to the Buffalo area tonight. I'm an iron worker and have to be on the job by tomorrow morning. Please help me!"

The trucker had a smirk on his face that told Hawk he didn't really want to take him on as a passenger. Hawk saw that and pulled out $300 in cash from his left pocket to show the driver.

He told him, "I'll pay you $200 for the ride. Please mister! I've GOT to get home tonight! Please!"

Hearing Hawk's desperate plea and seeing the cash, he figured he must be okay and not some guy wanting to highjack his rig. Anyway, he was packing a .38 revolver and has practiced pulling the gun out and firing if the need should arise. Truckers have been held up and this man takes no chances. He could see that Hawk was really stressed out.

He told him, "Okay, get on board! I'm on my way to Erie, PA and can drop you off anywhere along the way."

Hawk said, "You'll be going right past the area where I live in Irving, near routes 5 and 20." He climbed up, and as he did he said, "My name's Hawk."

The driver said, "Mine's Al." He rubbed his fingers together signifying he wanted his $200.

Hawk apologized, quickly counted out the money and handed it to him. He said, "You have no idea how much this means to me. I've been away from my wife and kid for over four months. I'm dying to get home. Thanks so much, man!"

Al smiled and said, "You're more than welcome. Iron worker eh? I was one in my younger days. I'm glad to help out a fellow 'sky walker.' I need a minute or two to check a few things in here and then we'll be rolling."

Before taking off, Al does one last check of; fuel level, air-break pressure, windshield washer fluid, windshield wipers, CB radio and making sure the parking break is off. As Hawk is watching him do all that, he can't wait for Al to put the truck in gear and head away from that service stop. He's so anxious to get home that it seems to him, every minute, every second they're standing still is lost time. He's having a hard time being patient. They'll be moving very shortly. Al is almost ready to go.

While Hawk and his driver get ready to move out, the men in the Crew back in the City have wrapped up their day and are headed home for the night. They're going to be very busy tomorrow.

CHAPTER 32

HAWK - HOME AT LAST

It's now 9:30 pm and the storm's intensity has diminished. Everything checked out fine in Al's rig. He puts it in gear and heads out. Fortunately, plows came through to clear away most of the snow and laid down salt. Still, he drops his speed down between 50 to 55 miles an hour, just to be safe. They're about four hours or so from where Hawk needs to go. This will be much better than getting let off in downtown Buffalo at the bus terminal. He'll be right in his own neighborhood, so to speak. They should be there by about one or two in the morning, depending on the road conditions. The visibility is a bit poor at times, but good enough for this veteran trucker to make decent time.

The two men share stories about the construction trade as the rig rolls along. They take turns talking about building projects they've worked on and the men who lost their life falling from high rise structures, losing fingers, limbs, or being crushed by steel girders. They both talk about the pain of being away from their family when jobs took them out of town for months on end to work on major projects. After about two and half hours, the conversations dry up and Al puts in a Beatles' CD. Now and then along the ride as they listen to the music, one of them has a question or thought about something and they get into short chats, then back to silence and the music.

When the rig nears Exit 77 near Pembroke around midnight, Hawk sees a familiar truck stop and his heart begins to race. He's not far from home, maybe another fifty or sixty miles. He figures he'll see the reservation in a little over an hour. The Thruway is clear of snow, but a bit icy. The truck moves along until they hit the Williamsville tolls, then the Lackawanna tolls. A half hour later, Hawk sees familiar surroundings. He's very close to home! The truck is low on fuel and the driver needs to stretch his legs. He takes the Irving/Silver Creek exit, number 58 and rolls over to a truck stop on Route 20.

The truck comes to a stop and the men get out. Hawk shakes Al's hand, hugs him and says, "Al, I can't thank you enough for getting me home. This is so great! I'll never forget your kindness. Thanks again!"

Al says, "It was no problem. Glad I could help a fellow sky-walker. You kept me company and I enjoyed talking about my days as an iron-worker. Take care my friend, and now get on home to your family!"

Hawk is thrilled to be standing on Seneca soil again and can't wait to see his family and friends. He knows his brother Alan is waiting for a call to let him know when he arrives. He heads to a

24 hour service station near routes 5 and 20 where his brother's son, Charlie works.

He walks in the station and says, "Hi Charlie! It's so good to see you! Can you call your dad and tell him his brother is here and needs a ride home as soon as possible?"

It doesn't take very long before Alan reaches the station with Hawk's wife, Diana. Her mother came over to take care of their son, Jacob. As soon as she gets out of the car, she bursts into tears and runs to him. They hold each other in a long embrace. No words need to be exchanged. They missed each other terribly and are overwhelmed with emotion.

Hawk, still holding on tight to Diana, says, "Baby, I'm so glad to be home. Not being able to be with you and Jacob killed me. Hardly a minute went by that I didn't think about you both. Let's get home so I can see my boy and talk to you."

They get in the back seat of the car like two young teens, just to be able to hold on to each other. Alan heads for their house.

As they ride along, Diana can't hold back the good news she has and tells Hawk, "Two days ago, our lawyers got papers from the courts that cleared you, Little Joe, and Martin of all charges. They came home a few days ago. And, more good news! They got their job back with the construction company. They told me that when you get home, your boss wants to talk to you about getting you back to work. Oh, and one more thing; the bar's insurance company paid for the damages. You're a free man John Hawkeye."

Hawk is beyond happy. Finally, things are going right for him. He tells her, "Thank God that mess got straightened out.

I'm so glad I won't have to worry about the cops coming for me. This is great! Now, I can restart my life. First though, I want to get home to see and hug our son and relax with you. Things are gonna be good from now on! You really surprised me with the good news from the lawyers, and you know what? …I've got a HUGE surprise for you! I can't say what it is right now. Let's get home and I'll tell you all about it!"

It's 2 am by the time Alan drops them off. As soon as he gets in the house, he goes upstairs to his boy's room, wakes him up and just holds him. His boy holds onto to him as tight as he can and sobs. He can't talk, he's too emotional right now.

Hawk tells him, "Dad's home for good son. I promise. No more going away and leaving you and mom, okay?"

Jacob squeezes his dad even harder and says, "I prayed every day for you to come back to us, daddy. I'm so happy you're home! I missed you so much."

They just hold each other tight. Diana stands by the bed with her hand on Hawk's head, watching him holding their boy. Tears are streaming down her cheeks. Her family is together again. She couldn't be happier. She wipes her tears and tells Hawk to stay with his boy as long as he wants. She heads to the kitchen to make him something to eat.

Hawk and Jacob talk for a while, then he tucks the covers around his boy, kisses his forehead and tells him, "I need to talk to mom, okay? I'll see you when you wake up, buddy"

Jacob says, "Okay daddy. See you in the morning. I love you."

"I love you too, son. Now, go back to sleep."

The surprise

He goes down to the kitchen, stands at the table and begins pulling out the cash from his coat pocket, from inside his shirt and then from both boots. He lays all the cash on the table …all $199,500.

Diana lets out a muffled scream and cries, "Hawk, PLEASE tell me you didn't steal all that money! You can't have the cops looking for you, now! Please tell me you didn't do anything bad! PLEASE!"

She's in tears. Hawk can see how upset she is and holds her till she calms down.

He says to her, "It's all good, baby! I didn't steal it. You won't believe how it happened. Right now, just believe that I didn't do anything bad to get this. It was a gift. I swear to you on Jacob's head! I swear it!"

He holds her until she's completely calm, then begins eating his breakfast before explaining about the money. He's done in about ten minutes. He then tells Diana the whole story. It's so incredible to her that she can hardly believe it. He pulls out the rolled up Saints cap from his coat and shows it to her, then the Saint Christopher medal. So that no doubt remains, he shows her the instruction sheet he still has.

After reading it; seeing George's name, the name of the bank and the amount of $200,000 dollars, she stands there with her hand over her mouth and says, "Hawk…you weren't lying! This is like a dream! I'm afraid I'm going to wake up to find I dreamt all this."

He says, "Sweetheart, it's no dream! It's for real and this money is for real. I don't know who the man is that put this whole thing together, but I would love to meet him to say… THANK YOU!"

It's very late. Hawk is tired and needs to shower. He tells her to go to bed and that he'll be with her in a few minutes. He picks up the money from the table and tucks it in a safe place for the night. He comes to bed and holds Diana until they both drift off to sleep.

CHAPTER 33

FOLLOWING UP ON... GEORGE, ROBERT AND BATES

On day five of this adventure, Jacques wakes up at 4:30, picks up Harry the locksmith and heads for Bates' precinct station. Frank, the desk sergeant's shift starts at 6 o'clock but he gets there at 5:30 and tells the sergeant on duty to take off. It's quiet when Jacques and Harry walk in. They're led to the captain's office and the locksmith goes to work. It doesn't take him long to open two cabinets.

Jacques looks through the files. They're alphabetical. He says to himself, "Druitt, Druitt, Druitt...come on, where are you?"

It's not in the first cabinet. He goes to the second and finds the "D's." There are several names in that section. Finally, there it is, Druitt, Dexter Michael. He pulls the file, opens the folder and takes a quick look at it.

He tells his partner in crime, "I've got it, the entire report I needed, with Bates' signature on the main sheet. Let's go!"

As they start to leave, Robert pops into his head. Bates has him under his power and threatening to send him back to jail. He goes back to the cabinet to see if Robert Xavier Greene is in the files. Lady luck is with him. He finds it and takes that one too. The men have what they came for and leave. Jacques stops by the main desk and tells Frank, "I owe you one."

"You owe me nothing Jacques. I still owe you for giving my son a nice cushy job in your company. He's doing really well and couldn't be happier. I was glad to help. Anything for you my friend and good luck with the information you got from the files."

The men leave the station and Harry is dropped off at his house. Jacques goes home and begins looking through the two folders. As he scans through Druitt's folder, he gets all the information he needs about his case and certain specifics that can bury him. He realizes that what he knows can never go public or reach his superiors. He also realizes that the victim, Miles Andrew Nevels is due a whole lot more than the $32,000 he's gotten so far. He figures that if there had been a trial for the hit and run incident, Nevels could have gotten at least a half million dollar settlement from the insurance company and Druitt, combined. He plans on speaking to Druitt about that to really make things right.

He opens Robert's folder and reads pretty much what he told Jacques and the others about doing jail time - "drug possession with intent to distribute." Jacques knows the courts have his records on file and that he can very well go back to jail if he violates his parole.

He also sees the judge's name in the records ...Judge Timothy F. Fitzpatrick. Interestingly, he contributed to the judge's re-election fund. That should be worth something. Having been part of high society for many years, he's made several acquaintances in high places. He plans on making a phone call to one of those acquaintances to see if the good judge would be willing to do him a favor on behalf of Robert. Yes, Rob Greene was involved in a thieving scheme, but he wasn't completely to blame. Bates gave him no choice, either do his bidding or go back to jail. Besides Robert, he also wants to see George and Druitt get set free from Bates.

Around 10 am, he calls Pete Savion, a friend of his in the court system and fills him in on Robert's situation. Pete tells him that he is a close friend of Judge Fitzpatrick and assures him that he'll take care of it. He's sure he can get Robert's parole rescinded.

With Robert taken care of, Jacques makes his next call, to the Knox Bank. He sets up a 1pm appointment with Mr. Ferro, the bank manager. He also calls Rick and Sergio to let them know what he's up to. He'll need Harry the locksmith for this part of the plan and will pick him up at noon in his chauffeured limo.

Bates' money

Jacques and Harry arrive at Ferro's bank at 12:45. They're announced to Ferro by his secretary. She says to them, "Please have seat, Mr. Ferro is with a client and shouldn't be too much longer.

After several minutes of waiting, the men are asked to come in to his office. Jacques tells Harry to sit tight until he can speak to the manager privately. He understands and retakes his seat. Jacques and Ferro chat for a few moments. He's a bit nervous. He tells Jacques that he's never had to do anything like this before. He understands that the money in Bates' safe deposit box is dirty, but he's hesitant about doing what he's being asked to do. It's illegal, and he doesn't want any of it to come back on him. He can't afford to be implicated in an illegal entry into someone's safe deposit box.

He tells Jacques, "This sort of thing is usually handled through a court order."

Jacques says to him, "Look it! If it should come out that you did this, you will tell the authorities that someone with a New York City police badge from Internal Affairs came in with court papers signed by a judge named Sparrow that gave him authority to open Captain Bates' safe deposit box." He adds, "I have a good friend who works in the court system that can get me those documents. I'll get them to you by tomorrow. They'll verify your story, but, it shouldn't ever come to that."

This relieves Ferro's fears. Jacques tells him that his locksmith is with him and will drill open the customer's lock and will replace it with a new one. They go to the vault. Harry has a satchel with the necessary tools to open the box. It's a large one. The manager is to stay with him to oversee what goes on. According to Harry, it shouldn't take more than five minutes to pop the lock. He was told the box contains extremely important documents. He's not been made privy of its exact content. It'll be better that he doesn't know. The money belongs to Druitt's bank customers, or their insurance companies.

Harry drills the lock on the box and as soon as it's done, Ferro escorts him back to his office and brings Jacques to the vault. He uses the bank's key to open the second lock, slides the box out, and leaves. Jacques is left alone to do what he needs to do.

When he opens the lid, he's amazed at the amount of cash he sees. He stuffs the money in a fair size duffel bag he brought with him. At the bottom of the box is a 3 by 5 inch black notebook. He takes that as well. Right now, he doesn't want to take the time to go through it. He'll do that at home with Rich and Sergio. Once everything is in the bag, the box is returned to its slot and Harry is brought back to install a new lock. He's done in ten minutes. The new key is given to the bank manager.

Jacques tells Ferro, "I have what I need. The box is empty. You can assign it to another customer. Bates will no longer be using it."

The men leave the bank and the driver drops Harry off at home. While still in route, Jacques calls Sergio and Rick and tells them to meet him at his place in a half hour.

CHAPTER 34

THE CREW VISITS GEORGE

When Rick and Sergio arrive at Jacques' apartment, he tells them that he's got the money and the files on Druitt and Robert. He gets ready to dump the money on the table to show them just how much Bates stole, but is interrupted by Sergio.

He tells the guys, "Before we deal with this money, I think we need to show ourselves to George to let him know what's going on. We know Hawk is probably home safe by now, but George is kind of just hanging out there. I'm sure he has a few questions he'd like answered and we need to be the ones that'll do that for him. For one thing, he probably figures Bates will still be gunning for him once he leaves the hospital. Let's do the right thing and pay him a personal visit to put him at ease, shall we?"

Rick and Jacques both nod in agreement. Jacques says, "You're absolutely right Serge. What am I thinking? Poor George, he's got to be going out of his mind worrying about leaving the

THE CREW VISITS GEORGE

hospital and having to look over his shoulder for Bates' guys. Let's go!"

The three arrive at the hospital at 4 pm. They go to the counter to see if Mr. Freemen can receive visitors.

The nurse tells them, "Yes he can. But since his surgery was so recent, he's only allowed two visitors at a time."

With a smile, Rick says, "You two go up. I'll wait for you down here and check out the lovely nurses."

Sergio says to him, "I'm telling your wife, Rick." Everyone laughs.

When Jacques and Sergio get to the room and enter, they find George sitting up watching Seinfeld (The Soup Nazi episode) … it's one of his favorites. As soon as he sees them, he's gripped with fear! He thinks they're Captain Bates' men. They can see how anxious he is.

Jacques tells him, "George, you have nothing to be afraid of. We're the good guys. We're the people who have been watching you for the last three days to make sure you and Hawk would be safe while you found each other in Times Square. We're the ones who set up the $200,000 adventure. Hawk's in the clear by the way. We caught a guy who was chasing him and took care of that problem. Your friend got on a bus for Buffalo and should have gotten home late last night. We've come to say that we're extremely sorry for what happened to you. It wasn't supposed to go that way. How are you making out?"

"I'm okay. It hurts, but I'll live. I'm so happy to see friendly faces." He looks at Jacques and Sergio in a reflective way and says, "Yeah, yeah! Times Square and the help I got when someone messed with me up in the spectator stand! That was your guy?"

"Yes. That was our man," says Sergio. "And when you were shot at, we were right behind the cab you and Hawk were in. We got hung up in a small car pileup and got behind in the chase. Once we got to where you were, the two of you were gone. But, we did catch up to the shooter. He pulled out a gun to shoot one of our men, but our guy was quicker and shot him in the stomach. We manage to get the name of the man who sent him before he passed out. It was…"

George quickly interrupts and says, "Let me take a guess … some police captain, right?"

"Yes, Captain Bates from the North Precinct. That's where you were placed for the night and released three days ago. How did you know it was a police captain?"

"I saw him in the bank talking to Druitt the day I got the envelope from your messenger. I went there to hide my half of the check so nothing would happen to it. I thought it would be the absolute safest place for it while I went looking for Hawk. So that's the bad guy, huh? It all makes sense now."

Jacques says, "I thought that was really ingenious George, you placing the check in the bank. I would have never thought of that. I'm impressed with the way you think! Excellent idea! Anyway, we came here to apologize and to assure you that you'll be safe. We spoke to the head nurse and were told that you'll be able to leave tomorrow if you feel up to it. We'll pick you up and get you to a very comfortable and safe place. In the meantime, we'll take care of Bates once and for all. After a week or so, we'll personally take you to the bank so you can withdraw your money if you'd like, and then take you wherever you feel you'll be safe. What do you say?"

"I accept your apology. But, the shooting wasn't your fault. That's on Bates and his goon. WOW! I've been going crazy trying to figure out how I was going to get my money from the bank and get to somewhere safe with it so I can start a new life. If you can help me do that, I'd forever be in your debt. I'm already in your debt for the hundred grand. Thank you so much gentlemen. Oh, one more thing… could you get me a new London Fog coat? Mine's got a bullet hole in it and lots of blood on it."

The men laugh and Sergio says to him, "We're more than glad to help, and…we'll certainly get you a new London Fog coat. Okay Mr. Freeman, rest now. We'll make sure no one gets in to bother you. We have a man inside who'll be watching over you. We'll send him by and he'll introduce himself. He looks like a doctor, white lab coat and a stethoscope around his neck. He goes by the name of Dr. Guiniache. He also has a scar on his right cheek. You can't miss it. Have a good night!"

George watches them leave. Jacques and Sergio made his day. He closes his eyes and finally feels at peace. He smiles and says in a soft voice… "Thank you Beau! I know you're watching out for your old man. I love you son! I'm gonna be alright now, you'll see. I love you!" He closes his eyes and his mind drifts off into happy thoughts.

As the men are walking down the hospital hall, Jacques says, "I'm still amazed that he hid the check right in the bank until he and Hawk got there. That's incredible! There's no two ways about it, I must hire him when this is over! *Il est un vrai génie!"* (He's a real genius!)

Jacques notifies his man (Joe) in the hospital and tells him to go to George's room right away and introduce himself. He does so and tells George that he'll be his guard for the night.

He locates the Saint Christopher medal among his personal belongings that were put in a plastic bag in the closet. He puts the medal around his neck and tells him not to take it off.

He tells him about the locator chip in it, and says, "I can't stay here with you all night, but if they should move you for any reason, we'll know and we'll be able to pinpoint exactly where you are at all times. You're safe now, rest easy."

George says, "Thanks a lot for being here. It makes me feel a lot safer. Good night Dr. Guiniache."

Realizing his boss let George in on the "Guiniache" name, he turns his head and smiles as he goes out the door.

CHAPTER 35

COUNTING THE MONEY

The men are now in Jacques' apartment and gather in a room where Jacques can have private meetings with clients when he's not at his office.

He empties the contents of the duffel bag on the large table, and the first thing that comes out of Sergio's mouth is…

"WOW! Will you look at that? This is HUGE! How much do you figure is there?"

Jacques smiles and tells his friends, "There could be as much as two million dollars, maybe more!"

Each individual little bundle has $5,000, $10,000 or $20,000 in it; in tens, twenties, fifties and hundred dollar bills. He asks each man to grab a section of what's laid out and start counting. They all get to work. It takes each man about twenty minutes to count and recount their stacks. Once done, Jacques asks for a tally of their share. Sergio tells him he counted $800,000. Rick tells him he has $750,000. Jacques tells them his pile of dough has $650,000 in it.

He does a quick calculation and blurts out, "Gentleman, there's $2,200,000 here! Bates and his crew have been very busy! The funny thing about the robberies, Druitt told me that of the money taken from his depositors, one theft was never reported to the police. Now, why would that be?"

Rick rubs his hand over his face and says, "I could be wrong here, but what do you guys think? Could it be that one of the people Captain Bates stole from is into illegal activities, and part of this money belongs to some very scary gang or outfit who hasn't caught up to him yet?"

Sergio says, "I'd be willing to agree with you, Rick. How can we find out?"

Jacques tells them, "I was given a list by Druitt of all the bank customers who withdrew large amounts from regular accounts and were robbed."

Then, he remembers the little black notebook that was in the safe deposit box. It's still in the bag. He put it in a side pocket of the bag after he emptied the box. He pulls it out and says to the others, "We need a list from a TV station that reported on people having been robbed of sizable cash amounts in the last three years. We'll compare that with Druitt's list of names and those in the black book."

Rick says he has a good friend named Gary Aeris who works at WNYC TV. He calls him and asks if he could get a list of people robbed of large cash amounts that were featured on his station's newscasts over the last three years. Gary tells him "yes," but that it would take him until about 6 o'clock to gather the information.

As the Crew waits, they talk about what they should do with the cash. Until they hear from Gary, it's a wait and see situation. In the meantime, they have no real idea what to do with all that money.

A little before six o'clock, Gary calls Rick and asks for an email address where he can send what he was able to glean from the station's records. He's given Jacques' email address and within ten minutes, they're able to print it. Jacques brings the sheet to the table and looks at the names.

He says to Rick, "Read me the names from Druitt's list while I compare and check off the names from the TV station's list."

He reads them off and it matches that of Druitt's list.

He then says, "Okay, now let's see if Bates' little black book has any other names."

Serge picks it up and starts reading it. Each page has a person's name, address, phone number and dollar amount. As he keeps looking through it, he sees a name that shakes him up a bit and says to the others, "Guys, one of the people in here is… Sam Danaroso. That would be, BIG Sam Danaroso!" He adds, "Big Sam is really a big guy; about six foot four and weighs somewhere in the neighborhood of three hundred pounds. This is a man people don't mess with. I know him through some of the building projects I was involved in around town. He's one of the big fishes around here! Gentlemen, I'd say our adventure is far from over! We have to look into this guy and see what we need to do. We'll be fine as long as we do the right thing. I'm sure

Danaroso's money is dirty. That's why it wasn't reported when he was hit by Bates' crew. The honest people who got robbed were probably able to collect from their insurance companies, but this guy, as far as he knew, his money was forever gone! His only hope of getting it back was to find out who did the stealing. Apparently, he was never able to locate the thieves."

Jacques looks at Druitt's list and can readily see that Danaroso's name isn't there. And, it's not on the list from the TV station. But, as Serge just noted, it is in Captain Bates' black notebook. The entry has $1,000,000 after his name.

He thinks for a moment and says, "Men, I think we have to contact our Mr. Danaroso to see what he has to say about his missing money. Whatever he says will tell us how we need to proceed in the matter. We'll need to be really careful how this is handled. We can't use any of our phones. We have to call him on an untraceable line."

Rick tells them that he'll go out and get a few prepaid cell phones. This way, Big Sam won't be able to trace the call.

While he's doing that, Sergio and Jacques do a breakdown of the amounts each depositor had. The search shows that Big Sam indeed had $1,000,000 taken and the rest, $1,200,000 of the $2,200,000 belonged to the honest people who reported being robbed. He hopes those good folks were able to get reimbursed by their insurance companies. He figures, if they did, they probably had to jump through hoops to settle their claims or were only given part of what was stolen. At any rate, this guy Big Sam Danaroso is a whole different situation, one that will need to be treated with extreme caution!"

CHAPTER 36

CONTACT WITH BIG SAM

Rick comes back at 7:30 with three untraceable phones. Jacques grabs one and tells Serge to read off Big Sam's number from the black book. He dials it, and as soon as one of Sam's men picks up, he asks to speak to Mr. Danaroso.

In a rough voice, the man asks, "Who are you?"

Jacques tells him, "Who I am is not important. Just tell Mr. Danaroso that if he's interested in the million dollars he lost a little over a year ago, that he should take this call!"

He's told to hold while he gets his boss. Big Sam gets on the phone and tells his caller, "Whoever you are, you'd better not be playing games with me! That would be a HUGE mistake! Who are you and where's my money?!"

"Don't threaten me!" says Jacques. "I'm not the thief who took your money, nor am I your enemy. I don't want anything from you. A situation came up that put your name and your money in my hands. I didn't have to call you. Your money could have stayed gone! Now then, there are people who were forced to get involved in the theft. I don't want them hurt. I don't have time to explain all the details right now. All you need to know is that I do have your cash and can get it to you by tomorrow noon. As for who robbed you, there's only one name I might give you if it becomes necessary. For the time being, you don't need to know. Understand that this man forced, and I need to stress … forced… people to do robberies. I don't even want to know what you might to do to him…if I give him up. If you should ever find out who else was involved, I need to reiterate strongly, they were not to blame! Can I have your word that nothing will happen to the innocent individuals involved in this?"

"Okay, you got my word. I promise nothing will happen to them. Now then, when and where can I get my dough?"

Jacques tells him, "I'll call you tomorrow morning between 11:00 and 11:30 to give you the exact time and location." He adds, "Mr. Danaroso, I know you're a very powerful man in this city and people know better than to toy with you. I don't want you for an enemy. I will do exactly as I said I would do. I WILL be in touch with you by mid-morning." He hangs up.

The men feel good about that conversation and hope that returning Danaroso's money will go well. They're a bit apprehensive. After all, mob type guys are not part of their inner circle. They're used to mingling with men and women who have normal careers; careers that don't call for carrying guns the way Danaroso's men do. Certainly, Big Sam must have friends and acquaintances that are very nice and charming, with talents and legitimate enterprises, but it's still a very different life from what the Crew is used to.

SERGIO'S BRIGHT IDEA

As they sit around trying to come up with the best way to do the money drop, an idea hits Sergio like a bolt of lightning!

He says to the guys, "We're going to give a whole new meaning to doing 'a drop.' We can't have Danaroso's guys see us. We have to do it in a way that nobody will get a look at us. My friends, we're going do it off the top of a building!"

Looking a little puzzled, Rick says, "Off the top of a building! What the hell are you talking about, Serge?"

He tells them, "Hear me out, okay? People in the construction trade know who has what projects going on, right? It so happens that I know where Danaroso has a vacant six story building he's been renovating. It's on Mulberry Street right next to a combination deli and apartment building. It has a trash chute that goes from the roof to a dumpster below. Since the drop is on a Sunday, no one will be working. We'll place the money at the top of the chute and get it to go down when it's time for Big Sam's men to do the pickup."

Jacques looks at him in amazement and says, "What a great idea! How do you come up with these things? Imagine that, one of Danaroso's own buildings. What a surprise that will be when I tell him where the drop will take place. I love it! So, who's going to be at the top to toss the money down the chute …you? They're probably going to send men in to look for whoever did it. How are you going to get out?"

Serge smiles, and says, "You guys liked the idea of the trash chute, eh? Well, you're going to love this! You know I'm a good fisherman, right? I can cast a line for a distance of at least a couple of hundred feet. Before Danaroso's men get to the building, I'll take one of my poles with a full reel of fishing line and fire it from the top of the building across the street. Then, one or both of you will be at the top of the other building to retrieve it, set the bag on the edge of the chute and tie the line to it. You'll have plenty of time to leave, and when Big Sam's guys get ready for the pickup, all we have to do is pull the string, and…down goes the loot! Of course, Danaroso's crew will think someone is in the building, and if they send guys up to catch whoever did it HELLO! Nobody home! Is that beautiful or what?"

Jacques gives him a big smile, turns to Rick and say mockingly, but sincerely, "Is he smart or what? I'm so lucky to be surrounded by intelligent people." He looks at Sergio and says, "Seriously Serge, that's a fabulous idea!"

Rick says, "It couldn't be any easier." Half kiddingly, he adds, "I'm very proud to know you Serge. You ARE a brilliant man."

It's all set. Jacques calls Big Sam and tells him the drop will be at noon tomorrow and that he'll call a half hour before that time to give him the exact location.

Serge goes home to find his best fishing rod and reel and give it a test while Rick stays with Jacques to take care of packaging Danaroso's money.

Now home, Sergio gets his fishing pole and goes in his huge backyard to see how far he can send his sinker-laden line. He wants to make sure it'll work the way it's supposed to. He readies the pole and lets it fly. It works like a dream. He's able to send it beyond two hundred feet. He figures the distance between the facing buildings on Mulberry Street is between 150 to 175 feet. He's very confident he can do this without any problem.

While Serge is testing his casting skills, back at his place, Jacques finds an old bowling bag to use as the cash-bag. He finds one large enough to hold a bowling ball, shoes and other items. He and Rick stuff the money in it. It's perfect, just the right size. With that done, the men retire for the night. Tomorrow should be really interesting.

CHAPTER 37

THE COOL DROP

It's 11:00 Sunday morning, day six. Jacques, Rich and Sergio arrive at Danaroso's building and Serge goes to the roof of the building across the street with his fishing pole. He readies his nearly $4,000 Daiwa MP3000 Angler Deep Drop rod and reel and gets set to make the cast. His only worry is that if he fails at his first try, it could be a real problem. A missed attempt would mean that it would go to the ground, and if there should be cars going by, reeling it in could be extremely tricky.

He's ready to go for it and says to himself, "Okay, Serge old boy, you got one shot. Make it count!"

Just like his practice run last night, he lets it fly and hits his target. He's very proud of what he just did and says to himself, "Man… that was world class casting! Boy, am I good or what?"

It was better than good. As a matter of fact, it was so good that it landed thirty feet or so beyond the edge of the building; over two hundred feet. Rick and Jacques were able to watch Serge do his magic and can see where the sinker landed. They find the end of the line and walk it to the chute.

Jacques feels a bit uneasy about being so close to the edge and gives the bowling bag to Rick. He tells him, "I don't do so well with heights. You tie the fishing line."

Rick cuts off the sinker with a pocket knife he always carries with him. Before he and Jacques went up, Serge had told them to do that before tying the string to the bag. The reason for it… if Danaroso's men happen to do any fishing at all and see a "sinker," they just might be able to figure out how the drop was done. You never know. At any rate, it's a good idea to remove it.

Rick ties the string to the bag and places it on the very edge of the chute. Satisfied it'll go down easy when they're ready to make their move, they make their way down and out of the building to join Sergio across the street.

At eleven thirty, Jacques calls Big Sam and tells him, "Mr. Danaroso, your money will be ready for pick up at noon at a building being worked on, on Mulberry Street next to Sacco's Deli. Your men will need to be in front and listen for a phone to ring. Once they find it and answer, that's when they'll find out where the money is."

"You GOTTA be kiddin' me!" says Danaroso, "That's one of MY buildings! I can't believe it! You're making a drop at one of MY buildings?! You've got guts! I'll say that much for you."

He tells Jacques to hold on a second and tells his men to go to the site Jacques just gave him, then gets back on the phone.

"Alright, my men are on their way. I owe you one 'Mr. Misterioso.' If all goes well and I get my money back, I'd love to meet with you...as a friend. I mean that sincerely. I'd like to buy you dinner to show my appreciation."

Jacques replies, "I'm not sure that can happen Big Sam, but hey, one never knows. Take care."

He hangs up and gets as comfortable as he can with his two buddies to wait for Danaroso's men to show.

It is a few minutes before noon when Big Sam's guys arrive. There are three of them, all tough-looking. As they get out of the car, they all have their hand inside their coat. It's pretty obvious why. These are three of Big Sam's most trusted men; Louie, Vinny and Stefano. Since they don't know what to expect, the men get a little distance between themselves so they're not clumped together. Basically, they're covering each other. Louie stands outside the car with his hand ready to pull his pistol if need be, and to also get in the car quickly and speed away with the others if they need to do that. Vinny stands with his back against the front of Sacco's Deli that is next to the building where the drop is to be made. Stefano places himself up the steps of his boss' building entrance. As far as they know, it should be a simple pick up and go. But, in their experience, men in their line of work have been known to be "set up" for an ambush, under the guise of "doing business."

Stefano peeks at his watch looking for the twelve o'clock mark. It's nearly noon. Since "the drop" was Serge's idea and, his fishing line, he gets to do the honors. Exactly at the stated time, he pulls the string and sends the bowling bag tumbling down the chute. He had already cut the fishing line from the reel and simply watched the ten or so feet he had left, slip through his hand as the bag made its way to the bottom.

Big Sam's men hear a thud in the direction of the dumpster that is about fifty feet away from Stefano. They can't quite pinpoint where the noise came from. Twenty seconds later, they hear the ringing of a phone. Jacques called it. Stefano walks towards the dumpster and as he comes closer, he can hear the ringing much louder. He opens the side hatch, sees the bag, opens it and spots the cell on top of the money.

He takes it out and answers… "Yeah, I'm listening."

Jacques tells him. "Tell your boss it's been a pleasure. And tell him that I can't take him up on the dinner offer, but I may be in touch for a favor someday."

Big Sam's man says, "I'll tell him. And …I guess it wouldn't do me any good sending my men inside the building to see who dropped the money in the dumpster, would it?"

"They'd just be wasting their time." says Jacques.

"That's what I thought. By the way, you did the right thing and handled this like a pro. That was good! So long, pal."

Stefano shuts off the phone, puts it in his pocket and walks to the car. He and the other two men get in the huge black Lincoln and head to their boss' home to deliver the money.

Once back at the house, Big Sam says to Stefano, "Everything go alright? You got my money?"

"Yeah boss. It couldn't have gone any better. We were out of there in a few minutes. " Lifting the bowling bag he has in his right hand, he says, "Got the money right here."

Danaroso, sitting comfortably in his overstuffed armchair and puffing on a cigar, motions for him to bring it over and set it down at his feet.

Sam says, "Good job boys. Glad we got it back. This million was supposed to go toward a deal I made with the Sabastian brothers for a piece of the action on that huge city project. Good thing I had enough on reserve to cover it. Boy, I'd love to know who did the heist! It REALLY bothers me not knowing!"

Stefano says, "Boss I still have the cell phone that was in the bag at the drop. You could call him back and see if he'd give up the guy or guys who pulled the job."

Big Sam says, "You still got the cell phone?"

"Yeah boss! I have it right here." He shows it to him and says, "I figured you might want to get in touch with 'La Volpe.' That's the name Vinny came up with after we got the dough. All you gotta do is look at the calls received and you should be able to get him on the cell phone he used to call this one. I'll do that for you, boss. It'll just take a minute."

The call is made…Jacques answers and hears Big Sam say, "How you doin' Mr. La Volpe?"

"La Volpe, huh?" says Jacques. "What does that mean?"

"It means, The Fox. That's what my guys called you after they got the money. My man Stefano told me how you did it. My compliments to you! That was very well done; no face to face contact, no surprises, just a simple drop. A literal "drop" no less! I've been involved in a few drops in my time, but I must say, doing it that way was both, a first, and quite ingenious. And…

just as impressive, you did it at one of my own buildings. I still can't believe it."

"The Fox, eh?" says Jacques. "I can live with that. I'll take it as a compliment. Glad you're impressed with the way I handled it, Big Sam. Now then, what can I do for you?"

"Well, it's like this. I very much appreciate you getting me my money back, but there's one thing that I can't let go …I need to know who did me the dirty deed. Is there any way I could persuade you to give me a name. I promise you I won't touch him or them. I just need to know. Not knowing will forever bother me. You know …it's a loose end."

"Mr. Danaroso, if I were in your shoes, I, too, would want to know. I understand how you feel, but I think I'll just hold on to that bit of information for the time being. In time, I will let you know. For now, the people involved must remain anonymous. That's all I can say to you right now. Have a nice day."

He hangs up, leaving Big Sam in suspense. Jacques figures that if everything can be smoothed over and everyone who is innocent in this whole affair will be safe, he might give him Bates' name. For now, it would just cause more headaches for him and the rest of the people connected with the whole affair. Before he can even think of giving up Bates, he and the rest of his posse still have several important things to button up.

Chapter 38

George safe – Bates released

On their way back from the drop, Rick reminds his buddies that George will be discharged at 1:30 and that they need to get to Saint Vincent Hospital. Joe, (Dr. Guiniache) took good care of him and called in the discharge time. Sergio heads to the apartment that he prepared for George while Jacques' chauffeur Ralph, drives him and Rick to the hospital.

They enter the room and see George sitting on the bed. He's all dressed and ready to get out of there. The nurse comes in with his discharge papers; he signs them, then all three men head out. They exit without any incident, but George is still a bit apprehensive.

The chauffeur is waiting by the curb with the limo door open. Joe takes over for the nurse who wheeled George from his room to the hospital doors. As he rolls him down the ramp and out to the limo, he can see how uneasy he is.

He tells him, "Relax George. You're safe and in good hands. All you have to do now is trust Mr. Blanchard and his friends."

Hearing that, George smiles and says, "Thanks Dr. Guiniache! This has been one heck of a wild ride for me."

Now in the limo, they head to a luxury suite at one of Sergio's high rise apartment buildings. It's a very secure place. He'll be safe there until the threat is gone.

They arrive and go into an underground parking area. The suite is on the tenth floor overlooking Central Park. The men go up and are met by Sergio. They get George settled in and post Joe with him to make sure he has someone to talk to and can help him with any needs he may have. The Crew wishes George good luck, say good-bye, and leave him alone with his body guard to enjoy a quiet and restful time of convalescence. Joe also needs to rest. He was on the job for a lot of hours keeping an eye on Georgie at the hospital.

What about Robert...?

As the Crew makes its way to the waiting limo, Jacques says to the others, "Let's see what we can do for Robert. He's due back home today."

They get to the warehouse and bring him to the interrogation room. He's still blind-folded. They tell him that he needs to call his wife to tell her that he got hung up; that he'll be in tomorrow. Rick calls the number and hands him the phone. His wife answers and Robert gives her the news. She's not happy, but understands that it's the nature of his job. The reason they had him do that is because they need to deal with Captain Bates first. They want to make sure he will no longer be a threat. Rick tells him they have to do something about Bates before setting him free. He'll have to put up with his situation a little longer.

Captain Bates released

The men bring Bates from his lockup handcuffed and blindfolded. They sit him down and Jacques tells him the way it's going to be…

"Captain Bates, I'm going to release you. You're through being a cop! You've hurt an awful lot of people. The best thing for you to do is to go to your office, put in your resignation and maybe even leave town. One of the people you stole from is an extremely powerful man that will probably make you disappear if we give him your name. I'm withholding that from him for now, but if it should happen that I do give you up, your life won't be worth a dime. I guarantee …this man WILL deal with you. Face it! You are a very bad guy!"

Bates knows the "extremely powerful man" is Big Sam Danaroso. He's the one that put his name in the book Jacques found in the safe deposit box. This puts a chill down his spine. He realizes that if Jacques gives Big Sam his name, he's a dead man! He says nothing. He knows he's done for.

Shadows Hutch and Everett take him to an abandoned pier in his precinct. He's still handcuffed and blindfolded. They let him out, walk him into a large shipping container and take off the cuffs. Bates hears one of the men chamber a pistol.

He's told, "Stay in here, and do not come out until you count to a hundred."

They want to make sure he can't get a look at them or the car. They shut the container door and push a 55 gallon drum against it, get in the car and speed away. Bates rips the blindfold off and counts to only seventeen. With great effort, he pushes the door open, steps out and looks around to make sure no one's there. By then, well over a minute has passed. Joe and Everett have had time to drive out of sight. He makes his way to where he can find a citizen with a cell phone so he can call a squad car to come and pick him up. He doesn't know it, but Hutch was let off after they sped away. He's following him from a safe distance and sends video to the Crew. About three minutes after Bates' call, a squad car arrives and he's taken to his precinct.

Upon entering the station, he doesn't talk to anyone. He goes directly to his office and notices straight away that one of the file cabinet drawers is slightly open. It's the one that should have Robert Greene's file in it. He looks for it, but finds it missing. He then looks through the folders for Dexter Druitt's file and sees that it's missing too. He knows who has them; the men who abducted him.

He sinks down in his chair and stares blankly at the wall. He resigns himself to the fact that he's been uncovered and it's only a matter of time before the man Jacques alluded to gets to him. He knows there is no way Big Sam won't kill him if his abductors give him up. He's tormented by the predicament he's in and searches for a solution, but it's no use. He comes up empty. He realizes that he's done for.

For several minutes, he takes a slow gaze around his office. He picks up the name plate on his desk and reads it, "Captain

Louis Bates." He then lays it face down on the edge of the desk and sits back in his leather office chair.

He keeps looking around at the different plaques, awards and commendations he's received over the years and feels proud of the good things he's done. He smiles. Then, as he thinks about how he broke his solemn oath as a cop, and how low he allowed himself to sink, he's genuinely saddened. His eyes well up and he feels the heaviness of it all. Finally, he forces a smile and shakes his head as if to say, "I started well on the force, and now, I'm ending my career, a failure. How foolish. It's over."

He looks at the front desk through the blinds of his office window, then.... a gunshot rings out! The desk sergeant on duty rushes over and sees Bates slumped over his desk. It is 5:45 pm. The news spreads like wild fire. Jacques' man from the precinct got the call about Bates' suicide and informs him.

Jacques can sense that his sergeant friend is bothered by it and tells him, "Look it! What happened isn't your fault, or our fault …it just became part of what he got into. You need to understand that Bates had several people by the throat that didn't deserve it. His own greedy actions got him where he wound up. Now, all those people he had under his power are set free. That's HUGE! You were part of setting them free. You did a good thing, Frankie"

"I suppose you're right, Jacques. Still, it'll take a bit of time for me to get over the shock. I'll be alright. Thanks for your encouraging words."

CHAPTER 39

ROBERT'S RELEASED

With Bates dead, the Crew feels that it's safe to release Robert. He won't have to worry about going back to jail. They feel really bad that he had to be deprived of his family for a few days, but felt that it was best for him to be kept in a safe place until they could get the captain off his back. With that done, there's nothing else to do but to release him.

Hutch and Everett again have the honor of escorting their next captive to freedom. They bring him from the warehouse to the area of the trucking outfit where he works. They stop behind one of the terminal buildings not far from where his car is parked and let him out. They untie his hands but the leave the blindfold in place.

Everett tells him, "Our boss wants you to know that he'll be in touch with you soon. Now, you're free to go home and be with your family. Be good!"

As the men get ready to get in their car, Hutch tells him, "Keep your back turned and wait until you hear the horn sound before taking off the blindfold."

The men drive away and as they make the turn around the building, Everett hits the horn. Robert rips off the blindfold, breathes in deep and just stares at the sky. It is beautiful! He hasn't seen anything for a few days and is taking in all that he can for a few moments. He gets in his car and drives home to his wife and children; thanking God that he's free from his captors, but even more thankful that he's free from Captain Bates.

CHAPTER 40

DEALING WITH THE EXTRA $750,000

Now, it's time to let Druitt know he can finally live his life without Bates ever bothering him again. Jacques makes the call and explains everything that's happened.

He tells him, "Druitt, you can totally relax now. Bates committed suicide and everyone connected to this mess is safe. There are only two more things to do. First, we need to figure out what we're going to do with the money left over after having given Big Sam what's his. We'll still have $1,200,000 to deal with. Second, Miles Nevels, the guy you hurt, I may have a way to compensate him without you having to foot the bill. The money that's left might just play a part in it. I need to check with the insurance companies to find out how much each person who was robbed actually got reimbursed by them. I have a feeling those policy holders got robbed twice, if you know what I mean. I'll get back to you on that. Take care."

He tells the guys that he needs to contact an insurance agent to get information on cases that have to do with cash being robbed, and how they compensate their clients.

Serge tells him, "I deal with large sums of money sometimes, and my insurance agent once told me that when people are robbed of cash, they usually have no hope of getting reimbursed by insurance companies. He said there's no way of knowing what people actually do with cash once they make bank withdrawals. It's way too easy to run a 'scam' on the companies. Anyone can say they were robbed and put out a number. How can it be verified? Quite simply, it can't!" He adds, "However, there have been instances where people got some of their money back, not much, but some. In cases of very reputable people who have bank records of taking out cash, then being robbed very shortly afterward, some companies are willing to 'go on faith, but…it doesn't happen very often. People with a lot of money often pay huge insurance premiums in case something like this should happen and can get a fair amount back, but never the entire sum."

On a hunch, Jacques calls Druitt at home and asks him if the people robbed were ever reimbursed for the money they lost. Druitt tells him that he has that information in his office and he'll have it for him in the morning.

Next day, 9 a.m. Jacques goes to the bank to meet with Druitt. He goes in and sees him alone in his office. He walks by the secretary and she motions him to stop.

He tells her, "Mr. Druitt is expecting me. I'll see myself in, dear."

She nods and he walks in. A cordial handshake is exchanged and the men get right down to business.

Dexter says, "I don't know why I kept records of what happened to those customers who were robbed. I just did. I'm a fanatic for details and record-keeping, I guess."

Jacques says to him, "You're a very efficient man, Dex. I'm not surprised you kept records on this. Let's see what you have there. I hope this will give me insight as to what I need to do with that $1,200,000."

Druitt shows him the police report of four of the biggest robberies with the amount each victim lost, and how much the insurance companies paid back to each claimant. He reads off the names and amounts.

Mr. William Harvey Reynolds $400,000
Mrs. Marguerite Catherine Woolworth $500,000
Mr. Robert Joseph Campbell $250,000
Mr. James William Worthington $350,000

That's a total of $1,500,000. According to the records, the insurance companies were as understanding as possible. These very important policy holders had been paying high insurance premiums to their companies for years. They got fifty cents on the dollar. That means Reynolds got $200,000, Woolworth $250,000, Campbell $125,000 and Worthington $175,000.

Jacques figures out that if he gave the victims the rest of the money from their original claims, there would be $750,000 left.

He steps back from those figures, looks at Druitt and says, "What's the guy's name you hit and have been making payments to?"

"Miles Andrew Nevels," says Druitt.

"So…what do you think my friend? Would Mr. Nevels feel rightfully compensated if we put that kind of cash in his hands?"

With great enthusiasm, he says, "I think he would be extremely pleased! This is a great solution! Thank you so much, Jacques! This is an incredible load off my mind. You have no idea!"

Jacques pats him on the back and says, "You're a good man Dexter. You made a mistake and suffered for it. Now, you can put all of this behind you. I will give you the money the four victims weren't covered for by their insurance company; you will in turn see to it that they get it anonymously. Just write them a simple note stating, 'Here's the rest of your money,' and attach it to their package. They'll figure it out. I'll take care of Nevels myself. Write down his address and phone number for me."

Druitt opens a locked drawer in his desk where he keeps certain very important folders, pulls out a file he has on Nevels, writes down the information Jacques wants and hands it to him.

As he was writing, Jacques noticed a photo of a man in the file and says, "Is that a photo of our Mr. Nevels?"

"Yes it is, Jacques. You might as well take it with you. I'll have no more need for it."

He gives it to him, the men shake hands and Jacques leaves to go home to plan how he's going to go about getting the money to Nevels.

Chapter 41

Nevels' Compensation

Jacques is very happy the meeting with Druitt went well and that he was able to get Nevels' address and phone number. Now, he's going to be able to bring closure to someone who truly deserves it.

Since it's still early in the day, 10:30 am, he calls Rick and tells him, "Contact Sergio and both of you meet me at my place. We have a very important job to do today."

Rick doesn't get a chance to find out what the "important job" is, Jacques hung up too soon. He calls Serge and the men make their way to Jacques' place.

At 11:30 am, the three men settle in comfortable armchairs and Jacques explains that the $750,000 left over after taking care of the bank victims will go to a Mr. Miles Andrew Nevels, a man who was not rightly compensated after Druitt did a "hit and run" number on him three years prior. He tells the guys how he suffered serious injuries; the loss of part of his right leg as well as other permanent injuries. He tells them that he lives on Cherry Street on the lower East Side.

He says to them, "We need to get him the money. The problem is that he lives in the Rutgers Housing projects on Cherry Street in building D on the fifth floor. We can't just drop it off and leave. If this man has anyone in the family or friends who find out about the cash and get greedy, it could be a really big problem! We need to call him and see if he's willing to come and collect his money."

Serge tells him, "You're absolutely right. Can you imagine a bad guy getting wind of what he has? I think it wouldn't be long before he'd get to him and take it all. What do you propose we do?"

Jacques says, "Before we do this, I'd like to feel him out a bit, find out what he's been doing with the $200 he's gotten every week. I wonder if handing him $750,000 would be a good thing or bad thing. I'd hate to think he might spend it recklessly, or be too showy about receiving it and become a target." He turns to Rick and says, "Hey Rick, why don't you use one of those cell phones you bought and call him."

Rick gets him on the phone and says, "Is this Mr. Miles Andrew Nevels?"

He answers, "Yes it is. Who is this?"

"Mr. Nevels, my name is Agent Clothier. I represent a firm that is aware that you were involved in a very serious accident a few years ago that caused you extreme pain and suffering…and the loss of part of your right leg.

NEVELS' COMPENSATION

"Yes, that's right." says Nevels. "It's gonna be three years this comin' June that somebody hit me and left me to die in the street! Why are you callin'?"

Clothier continues, "I was told that you've been receiving $200 a week from the man responsible for your injuries. I'm sure that money has come in handy. I don't mean to get too personal, but it's very important that I ask…what have you been doing with the money you receive every week?"

"Mister, I live in the projects and only get by on $1,300 a month New York State disability. It don't go very far. I don't spend it foolishly if that's what you want to know. I pay my bills and help my son with some of his college expenses with that extra $200 I get every week. We don't have much …but we survivin'."

"I'm glad to hear you're wise with your money," says Clothier. "I have very good news for you, sir. A man you don't know heard about the accident you were involved in and managed to acquire a settlement to compensate you. The reason I asked 'what you've been doing with your money' is because you stand to receive a very large sum as compensation for what happened to you. The man giving you the settlement money wants to be sure you will use it wisely. It seems you do the right thing with the small income you have. In that case, your benefactor wants to give you what you rightly deserve."

Nevels interrupts, "I appreciate that! Thank you very much. When and where can I get the money …and how much are you talkin' about?"

Clothier answers, "In order for you to get the money, you'll need to meet me at the Apple Bank tomorrow near Broadway and

Grant streets at 10 am. As for the amount you'll be getting, we'll talk about that at the bank. Just know that it is a lot of money, sir."

"Okay." says Nevels. "Apple Bank tomorrow at 10 am. I can do that."

Clothier says to him, "Now then, it's very important that you come alone. You don't want anyone knowing about this just yet, there's too much money involved. You can't trust anyone. You needn't worry about the cab fare. I'll be picking up the tab. Have the driver drop you off at the Broadway entrance. I'll walk you in and help you figure out how you want to handle the money; put it in an account at the bank and take only a bit of it with you, or take the entire amount home. The choice will be yours."

Nevels says, "I guess I have a little bit of time to think about all that, huh? I'll be there right on time. You can bet on that! You won't be able to miss me. I'll be the black guy walkin' with a limp. I'll see you in the mornin'. Thank you, sir!"

For Blanchard, Gage and Malich, this next item of dealing with the $750,000 for Miles Nevels was a most unexpected twist in their adventure. Never-the-less, it became part of it and has to be done.

Chapter 42

Nevels at the Bank

It's time to meet Mr. Nevels. The men leave Jacques' place along with two shadows at 9:15 am and head to Broadway and Grant. It should be an easy transaction. Rick and Sergio will stay in the car while Jacques goes in the bank to observe the proceedings without being seen by Nevels. Video of any action going on will be sent to the guys in the limo. Shadow Everett, acting as Agent Clothier will connect with Nevels when he arrives. The other shadow, Hutch, will already be in the bank with the briefcase containing the money.

Druitt, Jacques' banker from the City Businessmen's Bank has already contacted manager Willard Flick of Apple Bank and had him draw up papers for Nevels so he can open an account. It's all set. Everyone and everything is in place. After a ten minute wait, a cab pulls up with the client. As Nevels gets out, Clothier approaches it and pays the driver.

He says to him, "Mr. Nevels, how are you? I'm Russell Clothier, agent for the firm that procured the settlement money you are about to receive. Are you ready to have an extremely good day, sir?"

"I'm doin' just fine thank you, and…yes, I am ready to have a very good day. What do I need to do?"

"Let's go inside. Everything has been prepared for you."

He opens the door and as he walks behind Nevels, Hutch is waiting on the other side and hands him a briefcase. It was done that way so that Clothier wouldn't be standing on the street waiting for his client holding three quarters of a million dollars in a briefcase.

Jacques had the manager standing by. As he spots the agent and client, he leads them into a small conference room where Clothier can ask Miles privately, what he would like to do with his money. Once inside, agent Russ opens the briefcase so Miles can see what he'll be getting.

He tells him, "There is $750,000 here for you, Mr. Nevels."

As soon as he sees it, he breaks into tears and says, "For REAL?! Is this really for me? Is it REALLY $750,000?! I can't believe it!"

"Yes, Mr. Nevels. It's for you, and… it is $750,000."

Nevels takes a deep breath, still crying, and says, "Man, oh man! I can't believe this is all mine. I feel like I'm dreamin'! This is surely a dream come true!"

Clothier breaks in as he closes the briefcase and says in a gentle voice, "Mr. Nevels, what do you want to do with the money; put most of it in the bank until you can have time to think about how you want to spend it, or take it all with you today? I suggest you take a little for immediate expenses and leave the bulk of it in the bank where it will be safe. What do you think?"

"Mister, I may live in a poor part of the city and didn't get to finish high school, but I'm smart enough to know that kind of money belongs in a safe place. I'll take your advice and put most of it in this bank."

"Good choice! I'm glad I'm dealing with an intelligent man. A not so smart person might have wanted to do a foolish thing and not bank it. How much would you like to take with you today, Mr. Nevels?"

"If I could have a couple hundred dollars… that would suit me just fine. You see, I'm used to gettin' that amount each week as extra money. I'll figure out what I want to do with the rest later. I've been a prisoner in that damn project tower for too many years! For sure, I'm gonna move out to a one-story home so I can just walk out my back door in the mornin' and enjoy God's sunshiny days on good days, and sit on my front porch on rainy days. Glory to God! I can start livin' like a human man! Thank you mister! This is indeed a good day! It's better than a good day… it's a God-day! That's what it is…a God-day!"

Clothier says, Very well Mr. Nevels." He takes out a pack of ten dollar bills, peels off $200 and hands it to him.

Before the briefcase is closed, Miles just stares at all the cash inside, looks up at Clothier and says, "It's gonna be some good days from now on! My wife is a good hard-workin' woman. Won't she be surprised! No more work for her. And, my boy will be taken care of. He'll be the first in the family to graduate from college. Now, that's something big, don't you think so, Mr. Clothier?"

"Yes it is Mr. Nevels, and I couldn't be happier for you. You and your family rightly deserve this. Now, let's get the rest of your money safe and secure in your own bank account. Let's go see that bank manager and do the paper work, shall we?"

Clothier closes the briefcase and the two men make their way to Mr. Flick's office. They enter and have a seat.

The manager already knows what needs to be done and asks, "And…how much will you be depositing Mr. Nevels?"

Miles looks at Clothier as if to be searching to say the right amount, and Russ promptly responds for him, "That will be $749,800, Mr. Flick."

Nevels verifies the amount by saying, "That's right, $749,800 dollars. That's what I want to put in the bank."

Clothier hands the briefcase to the manager. He has one of his clerks come in so it can be taken to a counting machine to verify the amount. While the clerk is counting the money, Flick asks his secretary to bring coffee for everyone. As they chat, he writes in the amount on the bank documents for a savings account and waits for his clerk to give him the tally.

In about twenty minutes, the clerk comes in and hands Flick a slip with the amount he counted.

He looks at it and says, "The count is correct, $749,800. All I need now are two signatures, yours, Mr. Nevels as the depositor, and Mr. Clothier as witness."

The men sign the forms, and as bank manager, Flick signs his name. It's done! Nevels' money is safe. He's given a bank passbook with the recorded amount he has on deposit, and a copy of the document everyone just signed. Both men shake the banker's hand, they leave his office and make their way outside through the Broadway exit. Clothier tells Nevels that he will be taken home by one of his drivers.

Clothier shakes his hand and says, "Mr. Nevels, it was an absolute pleasure meeting you and helping you secure your money. I wish you the best." Handing him a card, he tells him, "And, here's a phone number in case you need further assistance with your account."

Miles says, "I thank you so much Mr. Clothier. This will forever change everything for me and my family. God bless you!"

Clothier pats him on the arm and says, "God bless you too. Have a great life."

He gets in the car and Hutch pulls away to take him home. Clothier had his mic on all the while so everyone could hear the conversation Nevels had with him.

That part of the added adventure is done. Jacques gets in the limo with his friends and heads home. All the men involved feel very good about the way this turned out. Now, there were just two more things left to take care of before the adventure was complete, helping Robert Xavier Greene and George Henry Freeman get settled in a new life of their own.

Chapter 43

Robert gets a new job

Robert got back to his family okay and made like nothing out of the ordinary had happened. His wife Cherie was very glad to see him back home safe. She saw on the news how treacherous the roads were in the Rochester/Syracuse area and had worried about him.

The following day, he goes back to his job and while driving his rig, he replays all that went on the past few days; having to take off work because Captain Bates ordered him to tail Hawk and get his money, being caught by Blanchard's men and being kept in some warehouse as a prisoner, Bates' suicide, and finally, his release and returning to his family.

These events made him realize that he was a very lucky guy. He could be sitting in prison. Instead, the man who got him into deeper criminal activities was dead, freeing him from the threat of going back to jail. Even though he's not a particularly religious person, he takes time to thank God for the way things turned out. His life was about to get even better.

After a couple of days, Rick had one of his men contact Robert and offered him a job as the manager in the shipping and receiving department. He'll go through a period of training, then in time, will be in charge of all orders coming and going. It will pay him $1,500 a week with benefits, that's $6,000 gross a month. His present job only nets him about $2,500 a month, $625 a week.

The work at Rick's company would net him at least $4,500 a month after taxes. That would greatly improve his life and that of his family. Besides that, Rick and his staff will be there to guide him on the job and help him stay on the right path.

Now, George

Although he has $100,000, George knows it won't last the rest of his life. Right now, he's set up in a nice apartment so he can mend from the gunshot wound, but once he's good-to-go, he'll need a job that will give him a good living.

Jacques knows this. He calls him at the apartment and says, "George, this is Mr. Blanchard, I want you to work for me as a supervisor in one of my garment plants. My people would train you and get you squared away in the job. Your salary will be $2,000 a week. What do you say?"

George is speechless, but manages to say, "Mr. Blanchard, I don't know what to say, except, YES! And... thank you so much!"

"You're very welcome George Henry. You just relax and get better. In a couple of weeks, we'll talk some more."

After receiving that bit of news, he hangs up the phone and falls on his knees. The first thing he does is thank God…

He says, "Thank you Lord for all the good things you've provided me. I'm truly blessed. Help me live a life that will have meaning and when you call me home to be with Beau, I pray I will have done things right."

Then, he begins talking to his son…. "Beau, it's dad. Thanks for seeing me through the hell I got myself in. I hope you can see me now, son! Like I promised you, I got cleaned up and I'm gonna be okay, more than okay. I've got a big chunk of money and a good job. I've done good Beau! Real good! I'm gonna live right and do you proud, son. You're always in my heart. I love you and miss you."

CHAPTER 44

WHAT ABOUT HAWK?

Now that Robert and George were taken care of, Rick mentions Hawk's name to his partners and says, "I wonder how Hawk made out? What'd you think? Should we send one of the guys to check on him and see what can be done for him – maybe a different job that won't be so dangerous or take him away from his family?"

The men agree. Jacques has Hutch fly to Buffalo to find out how he made out upon his return home. Fortunately, the Crew was able to get his address from George. He had given it to him during his visit at the hospital.

After landing in Buffalo, Hutch rents a car and drives directly to Hawk's place on Route 438 in Irving. As he gets near the house, he sees him in the yard playing catch football with his boy, Jacob. He finds it amusing that Jacob is wearing the Saints hat his dad wore during his New York adventure. He pauses and makes it look like he's checking his cell for messages, but is actually setting it up so the Crew in New York can hear the conversation he and Hawk will have.

As he makes his way closer, Hawk tenses up because the visitor looks like an "official" coming to do…who knows what? He's still a bit apprehensive after all he's experienced. As Hutch approaches him, he can see that he's a bit tense.

He tells him, "Relax Hawk. I'm here as a friend from the people in New York. My name is Hutch. I was one of your shadows. George sends his regards."

Upon hearing him say George's name, he relaxes, smiles and says, "Phew! I didn't know what to expect when you drove up. I'm glad you're a friend. How's my little buddy doing?"

"His wound is still mending. He's getting better and better each day. How are you making out Hawk?"

"I'm doing great! I'm back doing ironwork on the Buffalo Creek Casino project in downtown Buffalo and spending as much time as I can with my family. It's so good being home with Diana and my son Jacob over there."

Jacob has the football and Hutch motions for him to throw it to him. He does, and Hutch says, "Wow Jacob, you've got a great arm! How old are you?"

With the pride of a young boy, he says, "I just had a birthday last week! I'm ten. This is one of the gifts I got from dad." … pointing to the football Hutch is holding.

"Ten years old! I have a boy who's twelve. We play catch a lot too. You throw really well, son! Keep practicing with dad.

Who knows, you might even become a quarterback for the Bills! Wouldn't that be neat?"

"Yes sir, I would love that," he replies.

He walks the ball back over to him, puts his hand in on his shoulder and says, "Could I have a few words alone with your dad for a few minutes, then you two can continue playing catch?"

"Yes sir. I need a drink anyway. I'll be in the house and wait till you and my dad are done talking. Bye!"

Hutch walks back to Hawk and says, "Come on, let's go over and sit under that awesome maple over there and talk a bit."

The two men head over to the tree and sit on a bench. Hutch says to Hawk, "I'm glad you got your job back and that you're working on a project that will give you a paycheck for a while. What about when the project's done? What's next for you?"

"For now, I'm working close enough where I can be home at the end of the day. As for what I'll do when that job is finished in Buffalo, I plan on using some of the money I got to start up a combination metal and welding shop near here, that way I can be even closer to home and not have to travel far."

Hutch comes back with, "You're in your early thirties right now, but when you get older, welding might be pretty hard work. What then?"

Hawk says, "Oh, I suppose my boy Jacob will be able to take on the tougher jobs and I can busy myself taking care of the light stuff."

"Maybe Jacob won't follow you in that type of work," says Hutch. "Maybe he'll want to go to college and do something else. What do you think?"

"That's a very good point. I'd love for my boy to go to college and get into some kind of career, maybe law or medicine. He'd be one of the very few around here to do that. I suppose either one of those would be better than doing welding." Jokingly he says, "Hey, he could patch me up if I got hurt or sick, and if he became a lawyer, he could represent me in court if I got in a jam." Both men laugh.

Hutch says, "College would be great for your son, but our concern at the moment is you and your future. You know what? George and another fella that got caught up in the events that happened while you were in New York have been given very nice jobs by the men who started the whole adventure. I'm here to offer you a life-changing opportunity."

"What are you offering me?"

"Since you work on buildings and are familiar with many facets of the construction trade, how would you like to be head of maintenance and building projects for the casinos in western New York?"

Hawk is taken aback by this proposition and says, "Are you serious? How can you make that happen?"

"My boss has many connections. One of his very good friends spends a lot of money entertaining clients in western New York area casinos and has already spoken to the casino head man. We're prepared to send you for training in 'Building and Plant Management.' You would be involved in daily maintenance as well as present and future construction projects. The current manager is getting older and you would be his assistant until he retires in a few years, then you'd move up to his position. You'd be home every night with the exception of only a couple of days away at a time. It should only be a two month training period, and…you can take your family with you. What do you think, Hawk?"

"I think this is incredible! Thank you! Imagine that, me, the head of maintenance and building projects for the casinos. Can't wait to start training."

"Good! I'll report back to my boss and we'll get you started. So, get things in order and be ready to ship out in a week, my friend. By the way, your salary will be $100,000 a year." With a smile, he says, "Will that be enough for you to live on?"

Hawk comes back with… "It'll be tough, but I'll manage."

Hutch shakes his hand and leaves.

With that part of the Crew's business done and everyone taken care of, the adventure has just about come to an end.

CHAPTER 45

BUTTONING UP A LOOSE END

Just one more little thing… back in New York, Jacques being the kind of guy he is, tells his men, "I just need to call Big Sam and tell him something that will make his day." He tells Rick, "Get him on the phone on one of your throw-away cells."

Rick dials it and waits for somebody to answer. He hears a female voice and asks to speak to Mr. Danaroso.

She tells him, "My husband is having his dinner right now and doesn't like to be bothered when he's eating! You'll need to him call back in about a half hour!"

Rick says, "Well Mrs. Danaroso, tell Big Sam he'll want to take the call. It's about the name of a man who did him dirty. Just tell him that."

"I'll tell him."

Big Sam gets on the phone and with a bit of an upbeat tone, he asks, "Is this La Volpe?"

"No it isn't. Hold on, I'll put him on." says Rick.

"Mr. Danaroso, this is La Volpe. You'll be very happy to know I'm ready to give up the man who took your money. If you heard about a recent suicide on the news, that's your thief."

Big Sam says, "That's it! That's all you're going to give me?! Do you know how many people have committed suicide in this city in the last week? Come on! Give me a name!"

"Big Sam, that's all I can do for you. Just know that the man who did you that bad deed is no longer among the living. And… he being dead has liberated several people. It's all good. You got your money back, a very bad guy is gone, and several fine people now have much better lives than they had before. See you around, maybe."

He clicks off the phone, hands it to Rick and says, "NOW ...we're done."

CHAPTER 46

THE CELEBRATION

Since everything is buttoned up, Jacques plans on relaxing for a few days and then get back to work. But first…the celebration!

Jacques, Rick and Sergio arrange a private party for everyone who took part in this most unusual adventure. It takes place in a private room at a club Rick belongs to. Besides the "trio" who concocted the whole thing, the drivers and the eight shadows are present.

All the men sit around eating, drinking and talking about the part they played and replay certain events that happened.

Serge brings up George's idea of stashing his half of the check at the very bank they needed to go to. One of the shadows brings up the smart "decoy wallet" stunt George pulled off when he got robbed, and another states how blown away he was with his "salt and pepper" concoction when the young punks on the bus hassled him and Hawk about their Saints caps. That one got everyone laughing.

One of shadow Joe's favorite highlights was the incident where Hawk got harassed by a drunk because he was "Indian," and called him "Cochise." He liked the way Hawk knocked him out as they exited the bus.

Rick adds, "We can't forget Sergio's 'money drop' idea for Big Sam Danaroso. Now, THAT was absolutely one of the most interesting things we did. It was awesome!"

Jacques brings up the one thing that actually saved Hawk's money from being stolen. He says, "What George did was the most important thing that happened. Think about it. He was the one who spotted Druitt and the captain having a chat. He was sharp enough to spot the guy looking at him and Hawk once they got to the bank and went to overhear a cell conversation that brought up Druitt's name and the captain. And, the best part... his 'Plan B'. If he hadn't had that, to switch the cash with the pamphlets, and Hawk had walked out with the money, the shooter would have gotten away with it. He would have been long gone by the time we got to the site of the shooting, no need for him to return. He only came back because he stopped to check the bag and saw that he had been tricked. Having to come back looking for George and Hawk gave us time to get to the area where he shot George. I've got to give him top props. That bit of genius saved Hawk from being out $100,000."

Sergio says, "You're absolutely right, Jacques. We have to toast George for his cunning. He's the hero of this fantastic adventure! Men, raise your glass and let's hear it for George! To George, one of the smartest men I've ever encountered!"

Everyone in the room raises their glass and yells out George's name in an exuberant cheer.

After about three hours of reliving the adventure and socializing, Rick says to the men, "So, what do you guys think? Shall we do another adventure?"

Jacques stands up and addresses them, "Gentlemen, one thing about what we just experienced, it will never be forgotten. I appreciate all that everyone did. If I come up with another, I would love to do it with this crew. Let's raise our glasses and drink to George and Hawk. We owe them that for what they went through. And…let's raise our glasses to us for doing all the good we did for Druitt, Robert, Nevels and the people who were robbed. We did a lot of good out there, men. Good job! *Merci beaucoup mes amis!*"

THE END

About the Author

Roger was born in Magog Québec, Canada in 1946, moved to Welland, Ontario in 1955 and subsequently, to Orchard Park on April 15, 1959, then, to South Buffalo in April of 1960.

He attended South Park High School in Buffalo, New York. He received his bachelor's degree at Buffalo State College in secondary education (French and Spanish,) and attended the University of Buffalo for his master's degree in American Studies. After college, he worked for over twenty years as a full time French and Spanish teacher for Canisius High School, and part time at Medaille College - both institutions are in Buffalo, New York.

He is a singer and guitar player. He's written a 152 page autobiography for his family. He also wrote a book based on the story found in Luke 15 in the Bible entitled: "The Prodigal Son" (subtitle) "The Love of a Father" His third book is titled: "South Buffalo – The Way It Was" with the subtitle: "Life of the Baby Boomers in the 40s, 50s, 60s, and 70s."

CPSIA information can be obtained
at www.ICGtesting.com
Printed in the USA
FFHW022301060219
50418623-55630FF